A GARDEN WALL
IN PROVENCE

A Garden Wall in Provence

A love story about good bread, good neighbors, and the fickle winds of the mistral.

(Recipes Included)

Carrie Jane Knowles

Owl Canyon Press

First Edition, 2016

All Rights Reserved

Library of Congress Cataloging-in-Publication Data

Knowles, Carrie Jane.

A Garden Wall in Provence —1st ed.

p. cm.

ISBN: 978-0-9911211-7-5

2016-915226

Owl Canyon Press

Boulder, Colorado

DEDICATION

To

Jeff, Neil, Hedy and Cole

You've made my life a grand adventure.

The Fête of the Three Kings: Celebrated on January 6th, Epiphany, corresponds to the moment when the baby Jesus is presented to the Three Wise Men. This holiday is celebrated in the south of France with a special cake (gateau des rois) containing a small ceramic nativity figurine called a santon. The person who finds the figurine in his or her slice of cake is crowned king or queen for the evening festivities.

Gâteau des Rois: The traditional cake served in the south of France during Epiphany, which begins on Twelfth Night and ends on Shrove Tuesday. The gateau des rois is made of sweet brioche dough decorated with candied pineapple and cherries. It is similar to the King's Cakes served at Mardi Gras.

Santon: The word santon means little saint. These small ceramic figurines are produced in the Provence region of southeastern France and are part of the traditional Provencal crèche. In addition to Mary, Joseph, baby Jesus and the Three Wise men, there are various individual figures representing characters from Provençal village life such as the baker, the surprised peasants, the fishwife, and the shepherd.

Santons are baked into the gateau des rois, and the one who finds a santon in his or her slice of cake is crowned king or queen for that evening. Most Provencal homes have a crèche made up of these traditional ceramic villagers surrounding Mary, Joseph and baby Jesus in the manger.

Mistral: refers to a violent and cold north or northwest wind which accelerates when it passes through the valleys of the Rhône and the Durance Rivers to the coast of the Mediterranean around the Camargue region.

The mistral is usually accompanied by clear, fresh weather. It plays an important role in creating the climate of Provence. The wind can reach speeds of more than ninety kilometers an hour, particularly in the Rhône Valley.

MONDAY MORNING

Madame Reynaud woke up and, out of habit, rolled to her husband's side of the bed. Monsieur Reynaud had been gone already for ten years. She could hardly believe it. She swung her legs over the edge of the bed and slipped her feet into his old slippers. They were worn thin and at least three sizes too big. She knew it was time that she bought herself new shoes, ones that fit, but she had better things to spend her money on this week. Sunday was their daughter Monique's thirtieth birthday.

She went into Monique's room to wake her.

"The winter holidays are over, and now the children are going back to school," she said, pushing the shutters of her daughter's bedroom window open in order to let the pale gray light of the chilly January morning creep into the room.

"What do you bet Madame Kandel will be late, dragging her son Roger behind her like a donkey she is pulling to a trough? I can see her running now. Monsieur Duprés is in the schoolyard shaking hands and kissing everyone as they enter. 'Bonne Année, Bonne Année,' he calls to the children as they race through the door. Can't you just hear him, Monique, and see his little mustache dancing across his thin upper lip?"

Monique closed her eyes and imagined once again walking through that door and being welcomed by Monsieur Duprés.

"Ah, Monday. How I hate Mondays," Madame Reynaud said as she secured the shutters flat against the side of their house, careful not to let them clatter and wake their elderly neighbor, Madame Fleury.

Madame Fleury was ninety-two and had been ailing lately. Even when she was younger she had grumbled incessantly about the noise of the children in the schoolyard and just about anything else she could remember to complain about to anyone who would listen. Getting older had not helped her disposition.

"Guy Giroux's boulangerie will be closed today as it is every Monday, and I will be forced once again to go to Monsieur Boffard's horrible Tout le Pain for our bread. Tout le Pain, what a ridiculous name for a boulangerie. Apparently Monsieur Boffard is so ashamed of his own bread, he won't even put his name on his shop like a proper boulanger."

Monique did not respond. Every Monday morning her mother complained about the bread at Monsieur Boffard's, then went to his store, bought his bread, and they ate it. Everyone in Avignon, who lived in the tiny quarter of St. Ruf, always bought their bread at Monsieur Boffard's on Mondays because all the other boulangers on the Boulevard St. Ruf were closed.

"He is a lazy man," Madame Reynaud raged on. "I get there when he opens his doors, and his shop is cold. His bread is cold. I am sure he must bake his bread for Monday morning on Sunday evening, knowing all of us will be forced to come to him because Guy's is closed. And yet he stands there, selling his bread with a big smile on his face, telling everyone who asks that his bread is fresh! Hah! It is stale before I can get it home!

"The crusts are so hard, not even a dog can bite through his baguettes without dropping crumbs everywhere. Why do I bother sweeping my floors on Sunday? I should wait until Monday night, until the last bit of Monsieur Boffard's stale bread is gone, before I try to clean up! With the mess his bread makes, and the few crumbs from one of Guy's sweet cakes we have on Sunday morning, I could serve a feast for the birds!

"If it weren't for the tourists, who do not know what good bread should taste like, and Monday mornings, when all the other bakeries are closed, Monsieur Boffard would have no business at all!"

"Madame Fleury likes his bread," Monique said, sitting up so she could watch the children as they walked down the street. She closed her eyes again and tried to imagine them in the courtyard, pushing and talking, waiting for the bell to ring.

"Madame Fleury can be a fool for one so old. She thinks it is too far to walk down the block to get the fresh bread of Monsieur Guy Giroux. She also thinks the fancy awning at Guy's means his bread will be too expensive. So she goes to Monsieur Boffard and pays three francs for his stale bread.

"She should be more careful. I heard her daughter say Madame Fleury has only six teeth left. She pays ten francs each week for the coffee she has to boil to soak Monsieur Boffard's bread in so she can eat it. It would be better for her health and her pocketbook if she walked ten more steps to Monsieur Giroux's for a tender loaf of bread she could easily chew with her six little teeth!"

"Maybe she likes his bread," Monique offered, knowing it didn't matter.

"Who could like something so dry?"

"If you soaked Monsieur Giroux's bread in coffee, it would disappear," Monique offered.

"Precisely. His bread is tender. One does not need to soak it in coffee in order to eat it!" Madame Reynaud left the room.

The bell rang to announce the start of the school day, and the last of the children ran through the big green door. The mothers began walking up the street to shop for fruits and vegetables. Monique got up and dressed.

"So, Maman, what will you buy today at Monsieur Boffard's?"

"A baguette, I suppose. I don't feel safe buying his croissants. Besides, we had croissants yesterday morning. But tomorrow, maybe a brioche, from Guy's, of course."

"Of course."

"Have you dressed and brushed your hair?" Madame Reynaud called out to her daughter.

"Yes, Maman."

"Then it's time I helped you come downstairs."

She walked into Monique's room and placed her arm around her daughter's thin waist. She insisted on helping Monique walk down the stairs every morning. She worried Monique's bad leg, the one that had grown stiff from fever twenty years ago, might give her trouble. She did not want her to fall.

"Perhaps we should have a brioche again today. Put a little meat on your bones. I do believe you are getting thinner!" Madame Reynaud said.

"Not with all the sweets I eat. Between you and Monsieur Giroux, it is a wonder I can walk at all! I am so plump, I am like one of those fat dressed pigeons in the market."

"How I hate to see their little necks broken. They look so pitiful, lying there wrapped in bacon, their tiny silent heads bent close to their naked wings."

"They are so sweet!"

"Yes, sweet, but sad. How your father loved them. How much could two little pigeons cost these days? Perhaps that is what we should have for your birthday."

"Perhaps," Monique said, shifting her weight so the two of them were in balance with each other. She did not really need her mother's help but enjoyed the warmth of her closeness. "But there are other good things to eat, a bit of smoked ham, some sweet sausage, or even a little lamb chop or two."

"It is sounding like you are hoping for a feast for your birthday!" she gasped.

"How about a banquet?" Monique countered.

"A banquet," Madame Reynaud teased, "for fifty?"

"Fifty would be too many, perhaps fifteen."

"No, that would not be good, fifteen is an odd number. I would not like it if someone had to sit alone."

Madame Reynaud guided the two of them to the head of the stairs. Monique held the railing with her left hand and pressed her left hip against the curl of the cold iron banister.

"Madame Pécaut is opening the shutters to her garden," Monique said, closing her eyes to imagine the stout little figure of Madame Pécaut struggling with her housework. "Madame Pécaut has already had her breakfast and is now sweeping her patio. No, I don't hear her broom, I believe she must be hanging her wash."

Madame Reynaud laughed. "We're a little too set in our ways to be young or unpredictable anymore, aren't we? Perhaps we should have the name of our little street changed from Impasse de l'Alliance to the Impasse des Vielles. Dead End of the Old Ladies! It fits, all except for you and that odd little fellow Monsieur Duncan."

"Shh…," Monique cautioned, "something is wrong."

Madame Reynaud kept walking down the stairs, guiding her daughter as she moved forward.

"Nothing is wrong. Madame Pécaut is just hanging her wash."

"I do not hear the yipping of her little dog. In fact, now that I think about it, Charme was silent all last night. I meant to ask you about it earlier. Not that I enjoy the constant chatter of her dog."

"It was quiet last night," Madame Reynaud affirmed.

Madame Reynaud let go of Monique as they reached the landing. She went into the living room to fiddle with the heater.

"There's quite a chill this morning," Madame Reynaud said. "Should I turn up the heat?"

The strange silence caused by Madame Pécaut hanging her wet wash on the line to dry without the staccato yapping of her little dog bothered Monique. She knew there was more to the story.

"What has happened to our dear Charme?" Monique asked, coming into the dining room and taking her seat at the table.

"I had planned to tell you yesterday, but thought it was not a good thing to hear right before going to sleep."

"What happened?"

"First, let me say one can only assume the story is true because I first heard it from Madame Pécaut herself, but you know how excitable she can be and how she cared for Charme like it was her child. And, of course, to lose a child is a terrible thing."

"Yes," Monique agreed.

"But, the story is almost too fantastic to believe, which is why I didn't rush to tell you."

"Well?" Monique prompted.

"If you must know," Madame Reynaud pushed her seat next to Monique and bent her head close so she could speak softly, "Madame Pécaut believes Charme was eaten by a snake."

"A snake?"

"I told you it was too fantastic to believe! Anyway, Monsieur Duncan, who rents Madame Delacourt's house, told Madame Delacourt he was a herpetologist at the University, which is what Madame Delacourt told Madame Pécaut when he moved in. It is only right that Madame Pécaut should know who lives next to her.

"As you have seen yourself, Monsieur Duncan is young, and although he is balding quite badly in the front, he lets what little hair he has left on his head grow to all extremes and wears it in a pony tail down his back. It is rather thin and not too attractive. Madame Pécaut says she has seen him out on his patio on more than one occasion, brushing his hair like a maiden drying it in the sun.

"In any case, other than drying his hair out on his patio, Monsieur Duncan has not bothered Madame Pécaut, but Madame Pécaut's beloved Charme has bothered Monsieur Duncan. When Charme has awakened him in the middle of the night with her incessant barking, he and Madame Pécaut have had words.

"As you well know, once Charme gets going, she can get on your nerves. However, Madame Pécaut is alone, and Charme is all she has, so who can blame her for every little noise her dog might make? Perhaps if

Monsieur Duncan had taken the time to make friends with Charme, to feed her some scraps from his table or toss her a piece of stale bread every now and then, this thing would not have happened.

"But, to wonder what would have happened if two people would have been sensible about a thing, is to waste good thoughts, for, it seems, neither Monsieur Duncan nor Madame Pécaut acted sensibly."

Monique was anxious to hear more about the snake, but waited patiently while her mother spread out the story like fresh linen on their table.

"You have probably noticed that recently Madame Pécaut has started leaving Charme in the garden at night, and the dog has been barking."

"How could I not notice?" Monique replied, hoping to move the story along.

"Well, about two weeks ago, I saw Madame Pécaut at the butcher's, the one downtown where they have those tiny lamb chops they stuff with rosemary and mint, and she told me then that Monsieur Duncan kept snakes in his house.

"I didn't believe her, of course, but then she told me that Thursday evening, two weeks ago, Monsieur Duncan came home carrying a pillowcase that looked like it was stuffed with clothes. When Madame Pécaut saw him with this bundle, she stopped him and asked, as any good neighbor would ask, if there was anything wrong with his washing machine.

"That's when he showed her the snake."

"What snake?"

"The snake he was carrying in the pillowcase. It was one of the snakes from his laboratory in the University. He said it was sick, and he was bringing it home in order to take care of it.

"That is why Madame Pécaut began leaving Charme out on the patio in the evenings. She hoped the dog's barking would keep the snake from coming into her house. Madame Pécaut says she had read that snakes try to get into houses at night because they don't like the damp evening air.

"Well, the night before last, Charme was in the patio worrying a pigeon, or so Madame Pécaut thought. She heard the dog barking, then that little growling sound she always made when she'd cornered something like a mouse or a bird. There are so many pigeons in this city, it is no wonder Madame Pécaut did not think twice about why Charme was barking. Anyway, she was barking and growling and barking some more when Madame Pécaut heard Monsieur Duncan's patio door open.

"It was late at night, and Madame Pécaut never bothered to get up to check what was happening. Charme often barked and carried on if a pigeon had foolishly chosen to roost in her tree or under her eaves. Well, right after Madame Pécaut heard Monsieur Duncan's patio door open, she heard Monsieur Duncan call out to Charme the way someone might call to a dog if they had a bone or one of those little doggy treats to give them. And, instead of being alarmed, Madame Pécaut was relieved, thinking Monsieur Duncan had at last made friends with her dog. Well, the next thing she knew the barking had stopped. Which is what one might expect of a dog that has just gotten a treat and made friends.

"The next morning, when Madame Pécaut was returning from Guy's with her loaf of bread, she met Monsieur Duncan with his pillowcase. The snake, he told her, was feeling much better, and he was taking it back to school.

"As she does every morning, while she was waiting for her coffee to boil, she cut off the ends of her morning baguette for Charme. When she went out to the patio she discovered the dog was gone.

"So, now you know."

"Know what?" Monique asked.

"That Monsieur Duncan's snake ate Madame Pécaut's dog!"

Monique studied her hands for a moment. Just as her mother had said, the story was so fantastic, who could believe it?

"So, what will happen now?" Monique asked.

"Nothing, I suppose," said Madame Reynaud, getting up to put on her coat to go out to buy bread. "Madame Pécaut could find herself another dog, I guess. If it barked at night, the snake could be sick again. But, who knows, maybe Charme dug a hole near the rose bushes and escaped."

"Maybe," replied Monique. But, she knew, just as her mother knew, that Madame Pécaut's little Charme had been eaten by Monsieur Duncan's snake.

MONDAY AFTERNOON

Madame Reynaud had just come home from shopping at Les Halles and was busy telling Monique about her adventures.

"And, after you went to Les Halles, where did you go?" Monique asked her mother.

"Let's see, I took a right turn off the Place Pie into the zone piétons on Rue du Vieux Sextier."

"Why not on the Rue Bonneterie? Isn't that where the patisserie is?"

"Well, I would have, but some tourist had taken a wrong turn into the Place Pie on a bus lane and had come face to face with a bus. He and the bus driver were arguing over who should be the one to move. The tourist was asking the driver to please back up his bus just the littlest bit so he could get through, and the bus driver was throwing his hands in the air and shouting, 'Tourists, Tourists,' over and over again, striking his forehead with the palm of his hand.

"While I was waiting for the argument to settle, Valerie, from the Tourist Office, walked by and said none of this would have ever happened if the visiting driver had just come to their office and gotten one of their maps."

"Maybe I could get a job in the Tourist Office," Monique said.

"You don't need a job," Madame Reynaud said, raising her hand in order to caution her daughter to stop talking foolishly. She did not want to have yet another discussion about Monique's crazy desire to work.

"Maybe I want a job," Monique pushed, being careful how she said the word 'want,' hoping her mother would hear the need in her voice and be willing at least to talk about it.

"Madame Taulier says hello," Madame Reynaud continued, changing the subject.

"Did you get some candied almonds?" Monique asked, knowing the conversation about her wanting a job was finished for today.

"The smaller ones only. She wants too much right now for the larger ones. Everybody wants too much. They believe, just because the rich relatives have come to Avignon for the holidays, that everybody's pockets are lined with money.

"Thirty francs for a gâteau des rois, can you imagine? You'd think the Pope still lived here, and buying bread for Epiphany was a mandate from the Church."

Monique agreed with her mother that thirty francs was much too much for a small crown of bread filled with candied fruit and a china figurine. Besides, it was a childish thing, almost silly, the cutting of the loaf, the careful eating of the bread, each person taking tiny bite after tiny bite so as not to break a tooth or to chip the little china treasure lying within the pastry. Then of course, there was the paper crown made of gold foil. Whenever her father found the figure, he would wear the little hat as though he really had been crowned king. Regally adorned, he would then parade around the house for the rest of the day, commanding Monique and her mother to shower him with praise and kisses.

Even as a child, Monique had felt silly wearing the crown, but she always wished to find a santon in her cake. She loved the little china figurines and saved each one she found. Her favorite was the young man, hands raised to his head in excitement and bewilderment at seeing the baby Jesus. By now, she had a small village of santons, the china figures in the cake: baby Jesus, the wise men, two camels, and even an elephant, as well as the bright colored figures of the peasants, fish in their sacks, bread tucked under their arms, coming to bring their gifts to the baby Jesus. But she had only one angel. She had hoped this year to find another.

"I told Madame Taulier that for thirty francs, I could have a half dozen of Guy's best croissants or ten loaves of his good bread. Ten loaves!"

Monsieur Giroux also made gâteaux des rois, as did every baker in Avignon, but Madame Reynaud did not like the santons he used in his cakes, for they were the small ones from Apt and were not well painted. Madame Reynaud preferred the ones Madame Taulier used, the larger, better painted ones made in Marseilles.

She would never think of going to Tout le Pain to buy a gâteau des rois. Monsieur Boffard used silly little plastic figures that weren't santons at all but, instead, were princesses in long ball gowns that had no feet and, therefore, couldn't stand up on their own.

"Thirty francs is too much," said Monique.

"But what, I asked Madame Taulier, if this cake contains an angel? Or this one, or even this tiny gâteau over here, the one for only twenty-five francs that has three plump cherries decorating its top?"

Madame Reynaud pulled the cake from behind her back and showed it to her daughter.

"Twenty-five francs! You shouldn't have!" Monique clapped her hands in delight.

"Doesn't it look as though an angel could be hiding inside? Look at this little lump over here, or maybe under this piece of pineapple?"

Madame Reynaud was relieved no longer to be discussing Monique's desire to get a job.

"Twenty-five francs is a lot, but it was worth the chance that this year we'd find another angel. Besides, the cake is sweet, and there are only two of us. If I cut the slices thin, this cake could do for three, maybe four days, and then the twenty-five francs doesn't look like much. Not much at all."

"Thin slices would be fine," Monique said. "How is the weather? I was thinking I might try to go for a walk."

"The sun is shining, but if I am not mistaken," Madame Reynaud reported, "I could smell the mistral coming our way."

"No one can smell the mistral," Monique chided.

"It is such a cold north wind. They say it blows from Siberia, and I swear I can smell it coming as it winds its way down the Rhône River. I bet you your best santon, the little china shepherd you found in your slice of the gateau des rois at the fête of the Three Kings when you were ten, that it will be here before tomorrow morning."

Monique didn't want to bet. The mistral could blow for days, and if it did, the shutters on their little house would be closed, and she would not be able to go outside to look for a job.

"How can you be so sure?" she asked her mother, hoping to get her to doubt what she had smelled.

"When I left the house this morning the sky was blue, but the air was still. By the time I had reached the ramparts around the old city, the air was cool and felt as though it was raining, but it wasn't. You see, it was dry, but the air felt wet and cold and smelled of rain. The mistral will do that. It is like a calling card, a little warning he gives us that he is coming. Madame Taulier thought so too. She doesn't smell it like I do, but she hears it. She told me she heard it last night, that it woke her from a dead sleep with its far off whistling and howling."

Monique sat silently, straining to hear what Madame Taulier heard. To her ears, the sound it made was like a train bearing down on the tracks, its wheels screeching as it twisted and turned through the mountains to get to them.

"Do you really believe it comes from Siberia?" Monique asked.

"Where else could something so cold and lonely come from?"

"Yes," Monique agreed sadly.

"The mistral blew the night you were born," her mother began. It was a story Monique had heard a hundred times before, but she sat quietly, waiting for her mother to go on.

"We did not have a car then, no one did on our little street, and we could not get out to go to the hospital for fear the wind would knock us down and you would be hurt. We called the doctor and asked him to come. However, the mistral was blowing so hard it bent the trees. Your father was worried the doctor would not make it in time.

"The mistral is such an evil wind. If it had been a person that night, I believe your father would have gone out to fight it, for he was afraid it was keeping the doctor from our door, and he would be left to bring you into the world alone.

"When the doctor finally came, your father nearly fell down the stairs running to greet him. I would have laughed had I not been hurting so much."

"Yes, I know," Monique said.

"But, there is more to the story," Madame Reynaud said firmly. "The wind had turned the doctor's hands to ice. I was afraid the awful chill of his hands would burn your thin skin, so I had your father get two pillowcases and made the doctor put them over his arms and hands so he could catch you in a warm cloth.

"There we were, the three of us, the doctor up to his elbows in pillowcases, your father afraid to look or even speak, and me howling with the mistral. We must have been quite a sight, for it startled you when you at last came to us. You screamed and screamed and wouldn't be comforted until your father had bathed you and I had wrapped you up tight like a sausage in my warmest wool shawl. Only then, once your face was clean and calm and your little body still, could I see how beautiful you were with your shiny black hair and your sweet little mouth.

"The mistral blew for three more weeks that year, and you cried each night it came. When it finally left, you slept and never cried again."

Monique sat quietly listening to her mother, waiting to hear the whistle of the coming wind. When it blew, racing through the night as though it had someplace better to go, it made her head hurt. She wondered now, as she had wondered a hundred times before, if it really was the wind that had made her cry when she was born.

"Which is why I rushed home," her mother went on as though one story had ended and another was about to begin. "I will have to take our clothes to the laundry this afternoon, for they will freeze on the line if the mistral comes. Besides, I do not have clothespins strong enough to keep them from blowing away. Do you remember when the mistral blew Madame Fleury's underclothes into our olive tree and your father had to climb onto the garage and use a rake to get them down? There I was, standing in the yard, trying to catch her skinny old drawers before the wind could snatch them again from my hands."

"You could hear the shutters opening all up and down the alley," Monique laughed.

"We should have charged a fee for watching. But we saved them, all except for that one chemise that blew away before I could grab it. It was like a kite, the way the wind played with it, taking it up into the air, then letting it swoop down, then back up again. It was gone before anyone could do anything."

"Will you have to close the shutters again if the wind comes?" Monique asked.

"If I don't, the mistral will find its way into our house. Besides, with the shutters closed, I will be able to sleep."

The two women were silent. Talk of the mistral had brought a chill into the house.

"Let's have some soup for lunch while the clothes are in the washing machine. Afterwards I will go down and take my chances with the Gypsies at the laundry."

Madame Reynaud was afraid of the Gypsies. When she returned from the laundry, Monique was in the living room waiting to hear about her mother's adventures.

"Tell me what the Gypsy Queen said," Monique begged, pulling her feet up under her on the couch, bringing her knees up to her chin.

"As usual, she didn't say anything. At least not to me, but she was there, with her apron tied tight around her thick middle, her pockets full of coins.

"She always moves like a fighter, punching her wash into the machines. Today she had the whole wall of washing machines spinning at once, with more wash piled up on the floor waiting.

"The men were there too, the old one with no front teeth, and the younger one with sour wine on his breath. Something bad must have happened, for the Gypsy Queen didn't speak to either one of them, and twice, she went over to the old man and kicked at his feet."

"What did he do?" Monique asked, astonished that so much should happen at St. Ruf's only laundry.

"He got up and left, leaving the door open behind him. The Gypsy Queen ran to the door and pushed it shut. She pushed it so hard, I was afraid it would be broken and Monsieur Minot would have to install a new one."

"Where was Monsieur Minot during all this?"

"He is such a mouse! He was hiding in his little room in the back. He came out with a heavy wrench in his hand to see what was happening. But once he saw how much wash the old Gypsy woman had to do yet, he went back to his room and closed the door. A real man would have stayed and pretended to make repairs, so I would not have to be alone with the Gypsies. He even looks like a mouse.

"They say the Gypsies can steal with their eyes. Whenever they are there, and Monsieur Minot has scurried back into his hole, I stand in front of my washing machines so they cannot see our clothes. Which is why we have never had anything stolen."

"How could anyone steal with just their eyes?"

"Madame Fleury told me she was in the market at the ramparts one day, and a band of Gypsies passed her. When she got home, she discovered her earrings were gone. Gone. Can you imagine someone stealing your earrings right out of your ears?"

Monique touched her ears, checking to see if the small pearls her parents had given her for her sixteenth birthday were still there.

"She didn't feel anything?" Monique asked, astonished.

"Nothing. They were just gone. The Gypsies are so quick you can't even see them take things when they steal. But of course, Madame Fleury should not have worn her best earrings to the market. Everyone in Avignon knows the Gypsies will take your jewelry before they ever bother with your money."

"What did the Gypsy Queen have on today?"

"Rings. One on each finger. Big ones, with stones like I have never seen before. I tried not to stare, but I couldn't help myself. Over the knuckle of her thumb on her right hand lay a topaz the size of a square of chocolate, and on her left hand she had six gold wedding bands, and on her little finger, an opal dancing with fire. I knew from looking at her opal that the Gypsy woman knows magic."

"Why?"

"If you are dull witted, an opal will be cloudy. If you are bright, it will shine with streaks of bright blue and clear green, but if you know magic, it will crackle with red fire. It is even said that if your heart is black and you wear an opal, it will crack."

Monique thought for a moment about all these things her mother had told her.

"And on her ears?" Monique asked, wanting to know more, wishing she had been there to see this woman who could do magic.

"Big gold earrings that hung so low, they brushed against her shoulder when she turned her head. She also had on the gold locket with the thick gold chain she always wears."

"Did she speak?"

"Yes, of course, but not to me. She spoke to the men, and when Monsieur Minot came out of his hiding place, she spoke to him, but I didn't understand what she said, because she speaks quickly and talks in Gypsy talk, although it is cleverly disguised to sound like French."

"You must have been scared."

"A little," Madame Reynaud said, not wanting to frighten Monique. "But I am home now, and our wash is warm and dry. We are ready for the mistral when it comes."

MONDAY NIGHT

Monique woke to the faint cries of the mistral. It was three o'clock in the morning. She could hear the ripping snores of her mother's deep sleep through the walls of her room.

The shutters began to rattle, and the wind whistled loudly through the trees. Monique couldn't sleep. The thick flannel nightgown her mother made her wear, just in case the mistral came, was twisted about her legs. She pulled the heavy covers up over her head, but the roaring sound of the ice cold wind cutting through the long thin leaves of the olive tree in their garden made her clench her teeth. Her head hurt.

Monique lay in her bed and listened to her mother's heavy breathing. The shrill whistle of the mistral drove Monique to get out of bed. She put on her thick terrycloth bathrobe. Walking was difficult: the weight of the robe, along with the stiffness of her right leg forced her to have to slide her feet against the floor in order to move rather than walk properly. How she wished she could shake off the stiffness, spring from the bed and run down the hall to wake her mother.

It seemed like it took forever for her to go across her tiny room: her feet inching their way across the smooth cold tiles, her hands pushing against the rough plaster of the walls. But eventually she stood at her mother's doorway. She grabbed the doorknob so she could use her full weight to swing the door open. Just as she opened the door, the mistral cut across their alleyway and caught a dead limb from their olive tree, breaking it with a bright crackle and snap. Her mother didn't stir. An empty bottle clattered down the road, stopping occasionally as it caught a car tire here, or the base of a lamp post there, happy to rest a moment before the wind would come along once more to push it down the street. Monique shuffled back to her room and shut her door.

The wind laughed at her. Monique's shutters would be drawn tight until it left. She would not be allowed to go outside again until the mistral was gone and all was calm again in their little quarter of St. Ruf.

The mistral had crippled Monique. But that was a story her mother never told. No one ever talked about what happened that Sunday after Mass when she was ten and they went to the Palace of the Popes to walk in the garden. But she remembered. It was a sunny day, and she was wearing a thin coat and a fancy dress. They had eaten lunch at the little cafe by the carousel and decided at the last minute, because the sky had been so blue, that they should go for a walk in the gardens before going home.

It seemed like everyone in Avignon was in the park that day. Audrey, her best friend from school, was there. They ran up the sidewalks and snaked their way through the paths in the garden, hiding from each other and their parents, laughing and playing.

Without warning, the wind came. The sky, however, was still clear and so blue it hurt Monique's eyes to look at it. She begged her parents to let her stay a little longer so she and Audrey could keep playing.

Without warning, the wind got stronger. It began to tear at the tender spring blossoms from the trees. The three of them began to walk to the bus. Just as they came down from the garden into the broad open courtyard of the Palace, the little wind that had first whistled sweetly in their ears, turned into the most terrible of mistrals. It bit through Monique's thin clothes all the way down to her bones.

It was late in the afternoon and there were no buses in sight, so they walked the rest of the way home. At first Monique just felt chilled, but by the time they reached their home, the fever came.

The fever wouldn't go away. It stayed and stayed for many days until Monique no longer knew who was who or where she was. All the while, the wind continued to whistle and ring through her head so loudly, she couldn't hear what her mother was saying to her. Her small body tossed and turned and struggled against the fever.

Eventually, she was able to sleep tucked under the weight of her mother's best coverlet. The old quilt was so heavy Monique couldn't move her arms or legs and didn't stir. Nearly two weeks passed while she slept without moving as though she were dead. When she finally woke, her right leg was stiff and her heart so weak she had to be carried like a child again.

The wind outside Monique's shuttered world roared. The windows rattled as though the wind had twisted into strong tight fists determined to break the brittle glass of her bedroom window.

For twenty years the wind that had crippled her leg had whistled and laughed through her head and chained her life to her parents' home. No more. Starting tonight, Monique swore, she would fight against the mistral's taunting howls. She would hear it no more in her sleep. She would button her coat against its biting cold. Wind or no wind, it was time to leave.

She had tried to leave her parents' home when she was twenty, but her father wouldn't hear of it. They fought, but not for long. Shortly afterward, he became sick, and Monique believed their fighting had caused his illness.

Those were hard years for the three of them. Her father's illness spread through their house like a malevolent vine intent on choking them all. Just when Monique thought she could no longer stand to watch her father's body and her own life waste away, he was dead.

After his funeral, she waited like a widow until enough time had passed before she tried to go out in the world again. She was twenty-five years old by then and had never been beyond the walls of the Pope's Palace, had never made her own money, lived in her own house, or even shopped alone to buy her own clothes.

After six months of biding her time, Monique finally got up the nerve to tell her mother she wanted to get a job. They had just finished eating dinner. Her mother picked up their empty plates, took them into the kitchen, then went upstairs without saying goodnight. The conversation about Monique getting a job was over.

For the last five years, the urge to fight her mother had bubbled like a thick stew inside of Monique. But it was a stew that had simmered for so long, the fiery elements of it had long since mingled with the realization that her mother was all she had. If she fought her mother, she might lose her just like she had lost her father.

"Come in," Monique whispered to the dark window and the roaring wind. "Come on in if you dare!"

She took the long bolster pillow from her bed and stuffed it under her closed door so the cold wind could not race down the hallway to wake her mother. She pulled the heavy quilts from her bed and wrapped them around her shoulders. She twisted the latch and opened the windows to release the shutters. The wind ripped the shutters from her hands and filled her bedroom with its icy breath.

Monique covered her ears with her hands and closed her eyes. The wind stung her face and chilled her to the pit of her stomach. Then, just as quickly as the mistral had come in, it blew through her hair and raced back outside again and down the alleyway.

She closed the shutters, closed the window, and secured the latch. Her face and hands felt frozen. Her heart raced so fast it pounded through her throat and temples. Her legs were weak from walking. Her arms worn out from wrestling with the window.

She let her feet take their time to inch their way across the floor to the edge of her bed. She dropped her thin shoulders onto the bed and rolled across the mattress, causing the blankets to twist and wrap around her like a shroud. She shook her head until her long hair fell across her face like a curtain: it smelled of ice and wind.

She needed a plan.

TUESDAY MORNING

"Madame Fleury swears she heard the mistral tear the shutters off your window last night," Madame Reynaud said as she unwound the long wool muffler from around her neck and draped it over the hallway coat rack.

"It was a wild wind," Monique responded, looking away from her mother. "My shutters are still there, closed tight against the chill this morning."

"I hope you were warm enough and able to sleep."

"I slept," Monique answered.

Madame Reynaud filled the kettle for tea and then got out the two opened jars of jam: marmalade for Monique and apricot for herself. "We're almost out of marmalade. And, I'm sorry to say I forgot to get some when I went to town yesterday. Even more sorry, since you will be forced to eat Monsieur Boffard's stale bread again this morning. I hope there is enough jam to soften it and make it palatable."

"But, this is Tuesday," Monique said, a little surprised her mother had gone again to Monsieur Boffard's. "Is Monsieur Giroux's shop closed? Is he sick?"

"Oh, no, he is alive and quite well, and the windows of his little shop are stuffed with fat loaves of fresh hot bread and golden buttery croissants, but, as I was telling you, Madame Fleury did not sleep well last night, and when she heard me open our front door, she ran to the window and asked if I would be so kind as to fetch a loaf of bread for her. As you know, she only likes the bread of Monsieur Boffard. What could I do? I could not go into Monsieur Boffard's shop with a beautiful loaf of fresh hot bread from Guy's, nor could I go into Guy's with one of Monsieur Boffard's cold baguettes tucked under my arm, so I was forced to buy our bread again from Monsieur Boffard. If the wind had not been so terrible this morning, I would have walked around the block to be sure Madame Giroux would not catch me carrying these pitiful baguettes home. I had to hurry past her window as fast as I could so she would not see me."

Madame Reynaud busied herself for a minute setting the table. Monique did not say anything, for she felt sure the story was not over.

"You should have seen the smile on Monsieur Boffard's big face when I walked into his shop," Madame Reynaud continued. "'Bonjour, Madame Reynaud,' he said to me, 'I can see you have come back to my little shop again. I must have baked a good bread yesterday for you,' he went on as though I were there to buy bread for myself instead of for that silly Madame Fleury."

"What did you say?" Monique shifted a little in her chair, waiting to hear more.

"What could I say? There were people waiting in line, so I told him his bread had been particularly crusty yesterday, which was the truth! It got crumbs all over the table and even down onto the floor. I had to sweep twice to get them all.

"Then, as though we were good friends and I shopped there everyday, he pointed to a big sign hanging in his window about the fête for

Epiphany at St. Joseph's Parish."

"For the Fête of the Three Kings?"

"Yes! He points to the sign and says, in that big booming voice of his, as though he were having to shout over the whistling of the mistral to be heard, that he has been chosen this year to make the cakes. Can you imagine? Everyone knows he has the worst gâteaux des rois in all of Avignon. St. Joseph's should know better than to buy his cheap cakes for such a grand occasion. The Church is such a mess!

"Monsieur Boffard kept going on and on about his cakes and the fête, waving his thin baguettes in the air as he talked. People were getting impatient, but what can you say when a man is carrying on so? Just when I think he has finally come to the end of his boasting and is finally going to give me my two loaves of bread I have asked for so I can leave, he asks if I am going to the fête."

"What did you say?"

"I said, yes, of course."

Madame Reynaud pulled out the thin crusty bread and began to cut it.

"What happened then?"

"He held out two tickets as he handed me my bread, and now, not only have I been forced to eat his dry bread two days in a row, I have also been tricked into buying our tickets for the fête from him."

Madame Reynaud took the tickets from her pocket and laid them on the table next to the bread.

"You always buy your tickets from Madame Giroux."

"Unless I wish to buy two sets of tickets, I will have to tell Madame Giroux the truth. Perhaps she will see the humor in this situation. After all, she knows how I hate Monday mornings when I have to go elsewhere to buy my bread."

"What about the santons?" Monique asked. "Will Monsieur Boffard use those awful plastic santons for the festival cakes?"

"He says he has ordered special ones from Marseilles. But, who can believe him?"

The kettle whistled. Madame Reynaud went into the kitchen to make their tea.

Monique was secretly glad Monsieur Boffard would be the baker this year. If you were the one to find a santon in your slice of cake, Father Didier made you wear the paper crown and come up front to name your king. She would not be tempted to take even one slice of Monsieur Boffard's terrible gâteaux.

"Tea is ready," Madame Reynaud called from the kitchen.

Monique moved slowly, letting the weight of her body move her forward rather than the strength of her thin legs. The mistral had made both of her legs stiff this morning, and it took her more time than usual. Monique was grateful her mother did not come into the room and offer to help her.

When Monique sat down in her chair, she took a folded magazine from her pocket and laid it beside her place at the table.

"I toasted the bread for you," her mother said, placing a plate of warm brown toast in front of Monique along with a pale slab of creamy butter. "Monsieur Boffard's bread is even drier than usual. By the time I walked home it wasn't fit to eat. If this wind keeps up I am afraid we might be condemned to eat his inferior bread all week."

"It is very nice of you to buy bread for Madame Fleury," Monique said, buttering her toast.

"It is easier than listening to her complain. Besides, she is so thin and frail these days, one good whoosh of the mistral and she would be carried away down the icy waters of the Rhône."

Monique laughed, "The Rhône is two kilometers away. She is safe from the water."

"One is never safe in this wind. Besides, the mistral could grab onto the hem of that little blue coat of hers and fling her into the air like a kite. Off she'd go, up and down the alleyways like her old chemise."

"Shhhh," Monique warned, "Madame Pécaut can hear you!"

"Madame Pécaut hears our every breath. And, now that Charme is gone, she has nothing better to do than to sit in her chair all day long listening to our walls. I'll bet she can even tell you how many slices of toast I made for us to eat."

Monique giggled.

"It is true," Madame Reynaud swore, crossing her chest with her right hand and nodding her head.

"Perhaps if she got another dog," Monique offered.

"This is what I told her only yesterday when I saw her at the market buying vegetables. I suggested she get another dog, but she said she was afraid Monsieur Duncan's snake might get sick again."

The snake was a problem. However, Monique couldn't bear knowing that Madame Pécaut had nothing better to do now that Charme was gone than to listen in on their lives. It made the walls of their small house close in around her even more than the angry mistral.

"Perhaps a bigger dog," Monique suggested, "one the snake could not eat."

"Fantastic!" Madame Reynaud exclaimed, nearly jumping out of her seat. "How big would this dog have to be?"

Monique had no idea.

"Bigger than a rabbit," she guessed.

"Yes," Madame Reynaud quickly agreed. "I have read snakes eat rabbits. Bigger than a rabbit would be good."

"A snake big enough to eat a dog such as Charme must have been big. Big snakes have been known to eat pigs," Monique added.

"A pig is quite big."

"Do you think Monsieur Duncan's snake could have been a python?" Monique asked, trying to recall all she knew about snakes.

"Madame Fleury said it was big, and thick as the butcher's arm."

"I read once that a python can open its jaws and swallow a sheep whole."

"Something the size of a sheep would be a very big dog, indeed."

"Perhaps a Pyrenees, like the one Monsieur Duprés has. A snake couldn't possibly eat something as big as a Great Pyrenees," Monique said with confidence as she buttered her toast.

"A Great Pyrenees would keep our neighborhood quite safe from snakes. With a dog that big, Madame Pécaut would be so busy and happy she wouldn't have time to sit in her chair all day and listen to what we say."

Madame Reynaud unfolded her napkin and smoothed it out on her lap. She was quite satisfied they had just had solved the problem of Madame Pécaut.

"I have found something," Monique said to her mother, taking the folded magazine page from her pocket, "I want for my birthday."

"Oh?" Madame Reynaud said, peering over her toast.

"But, you cannot get it for me. I have to get it for myself."

"What is it?"

"A haircut."

"A haircut?"

"Yes, like this one."

Monique spread the magazine page out in the center of the table and pointed to the model's short-cropped hair.

"But her hair is blond," Madame Reynaud said.

"Mine will be short and black like hers is short and blond."

"Your father loved your long hair."

Monique started to say he was dead, but to say such a thing would be terrible, so she looked away for a moment, hoping her mother would understand.

"You will be thirty on Sunday. I guess it is time that you have what you want. Besides, your hair is so long, it takes hours to dry and so many strokes of the brush to keep it smooth. If it were short like this all you would have to do would be to rub it once with a towel and you would be ready to go. I can see why you would want it cut."

"Don't you think it would look pretty?" asked Monique.

"Yes," Madame Reynaud said, tracing the short wisps of the model's hair with her fingers. "When you were little, and your hair was just beginning to grow, it was curly like this," she said pointing to the picture. "You looked like a cherub that might have been painted by Giotto and put in the Palais of the Popes. Perhaps those curls have been hidden all these years, and when it is cut, voilà, they will come back again to dance along the edges of your face."

"So, I can get a haircut?"

"Where?"

"There is a shop on Rue Henri Fabré."

Madame Reynaud had seen the fancy shop on Rue Henri Fabré where the young women and rich ladies went to get their haircuts. This shop was different than Madame Soucie's on the Boulevard St. Ruf where she went to get her hair cut, rinsed and styled.

She had passed the shop on Rue Henri Fabré just the other day on her way to the market. The fees for the services were posted on the window, and it surprised Madame Reynaud that anyone in their right mind would pay so much to have their hair cut, but it seemed many did.

The shop was always busy with people sitting in the big leather chairs in front waiting their turn. The people she saw in the shop were the kind who wore fur coats whether the mistral blew or not. But there was no question that they looked like the blond woman in the magazine, as though the sun had just dried their hair and the wind had blown it around their face in neat wisps and curls.

"Are you sure this is the shop you want to go to?" Madame Reynaud said, looking at the picture again.

"I have heard they are the best."

"The best is expensive."

"It is all I want for my birthday."

Madame Reynaud did not want people laughing at Monique.

"You'll have to get dressed up," Madame Reynaud told her.

"I'll wear my blue dress," Monique said, smiling.

"You look very beautiful in that dress," Madame Reynaud said. "It is so cold outside. You'll need a fancy coat to wear as well."

"I have a nice coat."

Madame Reynaud nodded her head and thought: A fur coat could make the weakest of women feel strong against the stares and questions of the ladies in those shops.

There was no fur coat hanging in their closet. But, Madame Giroux had one. It was an old one, but it was a good one with fine silky pelts falling like soft black stripes from the shoulders. She would ask if Monique could borrow it.

Perhaps having the loan of Madame Giroux's fur coat to wear could be part of Monique's birthday surprise.

TUESDAY EVENING

"For once, I believe you are right," Madame Pécaut called out over the garden wall when Madame Reynaud wheeled her garbage cans into the alleyway for the regular Wednesday morning collection.

"About what?" Madame Reynaud asked.

"The dog."

"Oh," Madame Reynaud responded cautiously, for she could not be sure what Madame Pécaut had overheard through their walls when she and Monique were talking this morning.

"I've always wanted a big dog, but it was Monsieur Pécaut who insisted we get our little Charme. Not that she wasn't a sweet dog. She was, and such good company. I still wake up looking for her in my covers at night. You know, she slept under the covers by my feet and kept me warm. Ever since Monsieur Pécaut died my feet have been cold. I'm sure you feel the same about Monsieur Reynaud."

It was none of Madame Pécaut's business how she felt about her feet since her husband died, but Madame Reynaud did not want to distract Madame Pécaut from her story, so she bit her tongue.

"One could say that the feet of a widow are always cold," she said.

"Precisely. But a little dog is just a little dog and can't be much protection or even that much company for one who lives all alone. Don't you agree?"

"I am lucky to have Monique. However, the neighborhood has changed since the tall apartments have been built in Monclar. Madame Giroux said a gang of kids from Monclar tried to steal Madame Duprés' purse as she walked in front of their store the other morning. Can you imagine? There were two of them, one on a motorcycle and the other pretending to be waiting for the bus. When Madame Duprés came by, the one pretending to be waiting for the bus grabbed the handle of her purse and jumped on the back of the motorcycle and tried to drive off.

"Fortunately, Madame Duprés is a stout woman, and quite strong. She had her purse tucked securely under her arm and was able to hold onto it, but not before she was dragged halfway down the block to the gas station where Monsieur Courtine frightened them off with a mallet. He had been changing a tire, tapping the hub cap back into place, when he looked up to see Madame Duprés being dragged by."

"As I was saying about the dog..." Madame Pécaut began again.

"It would be nice to have a big dog, one big enough to protect all of us," Madame Reynaud offered; pausing patiently to see how big a dog Madame Pécaut was imagining.

"Have you spoken to Madame Duprés lately?" Madame Pécaut added.

"I called to see how Madame Duprés was feeling; as I was telling you, she was nearly robbed in front of Guy's the other day."

"It is not as safe here as it used to be, is it?"

"One must always be careful to carry one's purse tucked tightly under one's arm," Madame Reynaud responded.

"I always do."

"As you should."

"How is Monsieur Duprés' dog?"

"His dog?" Madame Reynaud forced a little surprise into her voice.

"He has a big dog. Big but friendly."

"Pierre? He is quite friendly. If Madame Duprés is going to be gone all day shopping or off visiting, Monsieur Duprés will bring Pierre to school so he won't be lonely. Great Pyrenees dogs do not like to be left alone. They are good company, and quite gentle with children."

"Does Monsieur Duprés' dog bark?"

"Like a lion."

"Where did Monsieur Duprés get such a dog?" Madame Pécaut asked.

"I believe he said he bought him in Gigondas," Madame Reynard offered.

"They grow a particularly sweet grape in Gigondas."

"When I talked to Monsieur Duprés the other day, I happened to mention Gigondas and their good wine. Monique's birthday is Sunday, and I thought it would be nice to have some good wine. Monsieur Duprés said he hadn't been to his favorite vintners in months. He has a particular fondness for the hearty red wine they make there."

"The wine from Gigondas is my favorite," Madame Pécaut said.

"Our talk about the wine from Gigondas made Monsieur Duprés quite thirsty. By the time our conversation was over he had made plans to drive there tomorrow morning. He usually spends Wednesday mornings working alone at the school when it is closed, but it is so cold this week with the mistral, he decided he would stay home. He said it was fortunate I had called, that a little trip to Gigondas would brighten his spirits."

"I have nothing planned for tomorrow morning," Madame Pécaut announced.

"Monsieur Duprés asked if I would like to go with him to get some wine. But I had to say no since I have to prepare for Monique's birthday. It is hard for me to believe she will be thirty on Sunday. It would have been nice to have a couple of bottles of good wine for her party. It is a shame I cannot go, but one cannot do everything."

"Perhaps I could go with Monsieur Duprés for you. After all, Monique will only be thirty once in her life."

"Would you?" Madame Reynaud asked.

"I have nothing planned. Do you remember exactly where in Gigondas that lovely dog Pierre came from?"

"As a matter of fact," Madame Reynaud said with a smile, "he came from the vintners."

WEDNESDAY MORNING

Madame Reynaud tried to sneak out of her house, but, as soon as she turned the key to lock her front door, Madame Fleury pushed open her bedroom shutters.

"Zut," the old woman muttered, clutching at the throat of her baggy terry cloth bathrobe. "The mistral blew so loudly last night, even though I covered my head with three pillows, I couldn't keep its noisy chatter from chasing away my sleep. Are you going for bread this morning?"

"Yes," Madame Reynaud said firmly, "I am on my way to Guy's."

"This wind has been the worst. My head hurt so badly yesterday, I could hardly eat a bowl of soup. When the light came through my shutters this morning, I knew, although I hadn't slept, that I must get up. All I could think about was how good it would be to have one of Monsieur Boffard's crusty baguettes to dip into my coffee."

"Would you like me to get you one?" Madame Reynaud called to the small figure in the window.

"You are so good to me," Madame Fleury said, tossing down several francs tied in a knot in the corner of an old handkerchief, "I told my daughter yesterday, when she called to check on me, that if it wasn't for your kindness, I would have passed away long ago. As you can see, I have felt so weak this morning, I haven't even been able to get dressed."

Madame Reynaud balled the heavy knotted handkerchief in her hand, fingering the coins. Madame Fleury was such a grippe-sou, she would never throw a handful of coins out the window for a three franc loaf of Monsieur Boffard's lousy bread.

"Can I get you anything else while I'm out?" she called to the wiry little figure in the window.

"A little warm milk would feel so good to my throat this morning."

"Demi-creme?"

"My doctor says I should watch the fats, that they are not good for my heart. A bottle of demi-creme would be fine. The grocery has a special this week on demi-creme, and also on those lovely little clementines."

"A couple of clementines?"

"If they are not too big, get three, otherwise, only two. This cold weather makes me so hungry."

"A couple of clementines."

"I will have to phone my daughter this morning and tell her again how good you are to me."

With that, Madame Fleury disappeared into her house, clanging the shutters closed behind her.

"Zut," Madame Reynaud whistled under her breath, stuffing Madame Fleury's money into her coat pocket. For the third day in a row they would be eating Monsieur Boffard's bread.

The clementines at the green grocer were a little bigger than what Madame Reynaud would call small ones, but then again, they were not too big. And since Madame Reynaud did not want to have to come back to the grocer tomorrow morning to buy more fruit for her neighbor, she picked three. The milk and clementines came to seven francs thirty centimes. She opened the knotted handkerchief and discovered Madame Fleury had given her only ten francs, which meant she would be thirty centimes short for Monsieur Boffard's bread. Who could ask an old lady for thirty centimes?

"Two baguettes," Madame Reynaud barked at Monsieur Boffard, "and two brioche, big soft ones," she said pointing.

Madame Fleury could break her teeth eating Monsieur Boffard's hard bread if she wanted, but she and Monique needed something softer to chew.

"I'm flattered," Monsieur Boffard said, a little too loudly. "If I am not mistaken, today is Wednesday, and this is the third day in a row you have come into my shop to buy my humble bread. Please," he said, stuffing two of the largest brioche into a sack. While holding the corners of the sack, he flipped it in his hands twisting the ends of the sack closed. "Accept these as a token of my appreciation."

Madame Reynaud was already down thirty centimes buying groceries for Madame Fleury so she graciously accepted the gift as recompense for her inconvenience.

"Are they fresh?" she asked, squeezing the bag with brioche.

"I have just now taken them out of the oven. As you can feel, they are still a little warm."

"A little."

"Will I see you at the fête at St. Joseph's on Friday?" Monsieur Boffard asked.

"You sold me the tickets, did you not?"

"It was my pleasure."

"I don't usually buy tickets I will not use," Madame Reynaud replied curtly, remembering she had yet to tell Madame Giroux she would not be buying tickets from her this year.

"Well then," Monsieur Boffard said with a smile and a sweep of his hand as though he was a young prince bowing to his lady. "I hope your prudence in the matter will become my good fortune."

"Au revoir, Monsieur," Madame Reynaud called out sharply as she left his shop.

"Au revoir, Madame Reynaud," Monsieur Boffard's big voice boomed out against the smudged surface of his closed shop door.

By the time Madame Reynaud got back to her house, Monsieur Duprés and Madame Pécaut were preparing to leave for Gigondas.

"How many bottles of wine," Madame Pécaut called out to Madame Reynaud as she approached them on the street, "shall I get for the fête?"

"There's to be a fête?" Monsieur Duprés asked.

"Sunday is Monique's thirtieth birthday," Madame Pécaut offered.

"I forgot to tell you yesterday," Madame Reynaud interrupted, realizing that by asking Madame Pécaut to buy the wine she had invited her to drink it, and now that Monsieur Duprés knew of the fête, she would have to invite him and his wife as well, "and was hoping I would catch you this morning. It is fortunate that you haven't left yet. I hope you and Madame Duprés might come."

"On Sunday?"

"For aperitifs at six," Madame Reynaud quickly decided. One couldn't have a fête without food, and a fête on Sunday would at least be aperitifs if not dinner. However, since there were now five in the party and Monsieur Duprés was known for his appetite, it would be best for her pocketbook if the party were confined to appetizers.

"And cake?" Monsieur Duprés asked.

"Of course."

With so many people coming now, she would have to order something special, which would give her an excuse to talk with Madame Giroux and clear up the misunderstanding about the tickets for the fête at St. Joseph's and to ask her if she might borrow her mink coat.

"Whose birthday?" Madame Fleury asked as she opened the shutters and leaned from her window, her bathrobe now closed with an old safety pin tight at her throat, leaving the rest of the raggedy garment to fall and flap from her thin shoulders like big broken wings.

"Monique's," Madame Pécaut answered.

"Whose?" Madame Fleury called out again, looking in Madame Reynaud's direction, her hand cupped to her ear.

"Monique's," Madame Reynaud answered.

"I'd love to come," the old woman replied, "at six?"

"On Sunday," Madame Reynaud nodded, holding up the milk and bread so Madame Fleury would see she had done her shopping for her and that she should come down the stairs to get it.

"Monique and I were hoping you would be well enough to join us."

"Your kind invitation makes me feel better already. Please tell Monique I am honored she thought of me."

"Yes," Monsieur Duprés added, "Madame Duprés will be delighted to know we have been included at such an important anniversary."

"Monique will be so pleased you are coming," Madame Reynaud said, shifting the loaves of bread into Madame Fleury's sack, so that she could free one of her hands to get her house key from her pocket and give money to Madame Pécaut for the wine.

"Four bottles?" Madame Pécaut asked.

"At least," Madame Reynaud did not want to appear cheap. The mistral, which had taken a small rest, began to gust and blow once again, lifting Madame Reynaud's scarf like a flag and nearly tearing off the thin doors off Monsieur Duprés' little car.

"It is too cold and windy to stand out here and count money," Madame Pécaut said, waving off Madame Reynaud's offer of money. "We can settle up when I come home."

"That is very kind," Madame Reynaud replied.

"It is the least I can do for Monique's birthday."

It was nearly noon before Madame Reynaud felt warm enough to go out and fight the mistral again. After she and Monique finished their second cup of tea with lemon and honey, she put on an extra sweater, her heaviest scarf and her warmest boots and coat and went out to do her own shopping. But, before she went to the market, she stopped to talk with Madame Giroux.

"Bonjour, Madame," Madame Reynaud sang out the familiar greeting as she stepped from the cold into the warm rich air of Guy Giroux's bakery.

"Bonjour, Madame," Madame Giroux responded, her tone a little icy, "I see you are dressed more warmly now than you were this morning when you went out to get your bread from the shop of Monsieur Boffard."

"Madame Fleury is sick again," Madame Reynaud started to explain.

"Madame Fleury seems to be sick a lot lately."

"The wind," Madame Reynaud offered.

"Ah, yes. The mistral. It not only hurts my head," Madame Giroux responded, "but my business and my pocketbook as well."

"One must make allowances for an old lady."

"You are kind to buy bread for her," Madame Giroux said, pushing her glasses up the bridge of her nose, her voice warming slightly. "Well, now, I am sure you did not come out in this cold just to talk about Madame Fleury."

"I came to order a cake."

"For a fête?" she asked, opening her order book.

"Monique's birthday."

"You must have scheduled your celebration for Friday evening, for it is the only good reason I can think of for why you have not purchased your tickets for the Friday evening fête at St. Joseph's from me."

"I am afraid I was tricked by Monsieur Boffard into buying my tickets from him. I knew you would understand, realizing how awkward it is for me to have to go to Monsieur Boffard to buy bread for Madame Fleury while she is ill."

"One must make allowances for an old lady. And, as everyone knows, you are very kind to her."

"I try my best to be a good neighbor."

"When is this fête you are having for Monique?"

"Sunday."

"A perfect day for a fête! As you know, Monsieur Giroux does not have to get up in the middle of the night on Sunday in order to bake bread for Monday morning."

"We were hoping you might come," Madame Reynaud said, trying to calculate how big the cake would have to be now in order to feed eight.

"Monsieur Giroux and I are delighted to accept your kind invitation."

"Monique will be pleased," Madame Reynaud said, adding Monsieur and Madame Giroux to her list. "We will need a large cake then, one big enough for eight."

"A good size cake indeed."

Monsieur Dudie, the butcher at Les Halles, had a good price on meat for pot au feu, and a fresh crock of his homemade rillettes, two of Monique's favorites.

"Some meat for a hearty pot au feu, and two hundred grams of your wonderful rillettes."

"Tell Monique I made it extra smoky just for her; the pork I used was some of my best, so good in fact, that I can hardly afford to sell it at this price, but I do not make rillettes for my favorite customers to make money. I do it to make them happy."

"She will be very happy. On second thought," Madame Reynaud added, realizing that a fat pot of rillettes would be just the thing to serve with the wine on Sunday, "give me five hundred grams."

"A demi-kilo! I am honored indeed; please, taste," he said, holding out a portion on the tip of his knife. "You can see for yourself, it is as I have said, some of the best I have ever made."

The smooth smoky flavor spread across her tongue like a dark sweet memory: a perfect match for the hearty red wine from Gigondas.

"I do believe it is some of your finest," Madame Reynaud complimented him warmly, "and will be the perfect thing to serve at the fête for Monique's birthday."

"A fête?" The butcher exclaimed, straightening his shoulders as he wrapped the meat.

"Yes," replied Madame Reynaud, quickly as she counted out her money, took her packages, and walked away before Monsieur Dudie ever had a chance to ask if he could come too.

WEDNESDAY AFTERNOON

When Madame Reynaud went into the kitchen at five-fifteen to put on the kettle for tea, there was a thunderous barking and shouting at her door. She also heard several loud thudding sounds, some more barking and shouting, all followed by the slam of a car door and the roar of a tiny engine as someone's car made a hasty departure from the curb.

When she opened the door, a large white dog leaped from Madame Pécaut's grasp over a barricade of boxes and into her hallway.

"Voilà!" Madame Pécaut exclaimed, throwing out her hands to show Madame Reynaud both the boxes and the dog.

"Wine for the fête! And our new pet!"

"There are four boxes here, not four bottles," Reynaud said coldly. "I do not remember asking for a dog."

The white beast was prancing in circles, frantically wagging and chasing its tail, trying to get close enough to Madame Reynaud to lick her hand.

"Yes, I know, however, when I was in Gigondas this afternoon, I remembered how concerned you have been of late for your and Monique's safety, and it occurred to me that a dog, like the one we have here, one that is big enough to guard both of our houses, one big enough that a snake cannot devour it, one that will grow into a fine watchdog, is a dog that is big enough to be shared."

"Grow?" Madame Reynaud said incredulously, watching the tail of the dog swing in a beating rhythm against the hall table where she kept her telephone: the receiver rocking in its cradle at each exacting swish.

"Pantagruel is but a puppy, only six months old, and as you can tell by his feet, he promises to be quite the dog for us, indeed."

"Pantagruel?"

"His father was Gargantua. It seems the breeder is a fan of Rabelais."

"And the mother?"

"A sweet little thing named Posey, with a gray mark across her face, much like the one Pantagruel has, see," Madame Pécaut said, pointing to the rather large gray splotch that covered the eyes and one ear of Pantagruel. "It is a beautiful mark. A prize-winning dog for sure!"

Madame Reynaud doubted Pantagruel's ability to win any prizes, but prizes were not in question at the moment: ownership was.

"I do not want a dog in my house," Madame Reynaud said with firm resolve.

"Perhaps that is not what you wanted when you asked me to go to Gigandas for you to buy some wine. But you needed wine for your fête and I wanted a dog to replace my dear Charme, and, as you pointed out to me, it would have to be a large dog, a dog big enough not to be eaten by Monsieur Duncan's snake.

"When Monsieur Duprés took me to the vintner, who had both the best wine in Gigondas as well as the best Great Pyrenees, it was simply a matter of getting the best deal for both of us. If I had gotten only four bottles of wine for you, you might not have had enough wine for your fête, and the dog would have cost me a thousand francs.

"Because you bought four cases of wine for your fête, the dog was practically free! He cost five hundred francs, which is not much at all for a dog big enough for two people to share, and, the vintner gave me a good deal on the wine, as well.

"If I would have bought you only four bottles, you would have had to pay twenty francs a bottle. By buying four cases, the wine was only fifteen francs a bottle.

"You now have plenty of wine for your fête at a good price, and we both have the protection of this fine dog. I will keep Pantagruel at my house, and we will both have what we want, will we not?" Madame Pécaut said with a smile.

"You are right," Madame Reynaud said, taking her purse from its hook and writing a check for the wine as quickly as she could so Madame Pécaut would take Pantagruel home with her. "It is a very good price for very good wine, and as I can see for myself, you have gotten the perfect dog to keep all of us safe from snakes."

"I thought you might agree," Madame Pécaut said, pushing the four heavy boxes into Madame Reynaud's now muddy hallway. "Come along, Panta," she called, slapping her hands together and motioning for the dog to come.

As he heard his name, the wagging and prancing stopped, and in one surprisingly fluid leap, the dog cleared all four boxes, landing gracefully at the side of his new owner, Madame Pécaut.

THURSDAY MORNING

Pantagruel barked all night long. In fact, the night had gone so badly, Madame Reynaud wiped any foolish thoughts she had of buying a good loaf of bread from Guy Giroux's right out of her mind.

"Madame Fleury," she called out to her neighbor as she knocked on her door, "I am going for bread. Shall I get you a baguette from Monsieur Boffard?"

Madame Fleury's bedroom window shutters flew open.

"I have heard that the dog of Madame Pécaut is so big there is no chance a snake could eat it. Is that so?"

"I am afraid that is so."

"It looks a little like a bear."

"I know."

"But barks like a dog."

"That it does."

"All night long."

"A baguette?" Madame Reynaud asked.

"I grew so weary during the night that I woke with a start at three o'clock realizing the barking had stopped. I was so amazed, I went to my window and opened the shutters, expecting without a doubt to see a large snake struggling to get over Madame Pécaut's fence. But, alas, there was no snake and as I opened the shutters the dog awoke and began barking again."

"A burglar would be a fool to come near our street."

"I have never seen a dog so big."

"He is but a puppy."

"Zut," the old woman muttered under her breath. "Do you think she'll let him sleep inside tonight?"

"Perhaps she will put him in the garage," Madame Reynaud offered weakly, not wanting to talk anymore about the barking dog she had helped bring into their lives.

"It is a good thing Madame Pécaut has a garage," Madame Fleury said.

"A very good thing. A baguette from Monsieur Boffard's?"

"I am afraid I am so weak again this morning that a baguette is all I can manage. I would go myself if I could, just to get away from that dog. I talked to my doctor yesterday on the phone, and he said I must eat. I am old and weak and the only thing that will save me is food, so if you could, would you also get a little round of goat cheese from the market next to Monsieur Boffard's. Their cheese is the best and always fresh. Be sure it is fresh, and not one of those that has been allowed to sit and turn blue with mold at the edges. Perhaps a ripe banana or two, if they are small."

Madame Fleury counted out her money and tied it securely in the corner of her old handkerchief. She threw it out her window down to Madame Reynaud.

"A goat cheese, two bananas and a baguette, are you sure that is enough?" Madame Reynaud asked, fingering the money to see how much there was, and therefore how much more Madame Fleury wanted from her.

"I hate to ask, but as the doctor said the only thing that would save me was food, could you possibly get a scoop or two of prunes? I do not like the ones that sit on the top of the container for they are hard. If you could, dig down to the bottom and get me a handful or two of the softest ones. I like the larger ones for they are sweeter and not so difficult for me to chew. A hundred grams or so is what I need."

"A hundred grams of prunes."

"There is plenty of money in the handkerchief to pay for everything," Madame Fleury offered.

"I have no doubt."

"If you happen to go to buy the cheese first, and you have a few francs left over, it would be so good to have one of Monsieur's soft croissants to eat with tea this afternoon. If you wouldn't mind."

"Why would I mind?" Madame Reynaud closed her hand around the knotted handkerchief and put it in her pocket, satisfied that the list was at last complete.

"It makes me hungry just to think of all the delicious things you will bring me!"

"Au revoir."

"Au revoir, and merci," Madame Fleury replied as she pulled her shutters closed.

When Madame Reynaud reached the corner, the money in her pocket gave her an idea. Madame Fleury had wanted a soft croissant. She could go to Guy Giroux's for croissants for Monique and herself, then hide them from Monsieur Boffard in her purse. While she was at Guy's, she could ask Madame Giroux if Monique might not borrow her fur coat so she could be properly dressed to go to the fancy shop for her birthday haircut.

Since they had invited themselves to her party, the least Madame Giroux could do was lend her the coat.

"Bonjour, Madame," Madame Reynaud greeted Madame Giroux.

"Bonjour, Madame," Madame Giroux replied.

"Two croissants," Madame Reynaud ordered.

"And a baguette?" Madame Giroux asked.

"No baguette today, just the croissants."

"How could two croissants possibly be enough for you and Monique?"

"How could we eat more with the wind blowing so loudly in our ears?"

"When the mistral threatens us, it is even more important to eat well."

"Two croissants," Madame Reynaud stood firm.

"Then two croissants it shall be, but if you get hungry by ten o'clock, don't blame me, for I tried my best to sell you the bread you need."

"I need to ask a favor, not for me, but for Monique."

"Ask," Madame Giroux said, putting the two plump croissants into a bag and folding the top closed.

"As you know, Monique is having a birthday this week, her thirtieth."

"Monsieur Giroux was so pleased to be invited. He is creating something special for her fête: a chocolate gateau made with sweet butter cream and raspberries. It is one of his finest and most expensive cakes. Since you were so kind as to invite us, and there will be so many at the fête, I changed your order slightly. We wanted to bring you the best we made. I meant to tell you, but I have not seen you since you came in to place your order."

"I placed the order yesterday," Madame Reynaud said, a little annoyed Madame Giroux, like Madame Pécaut, would take such liberties with her money.

"Ah, yes," she said checking her order book. "It was yesterday, but since you have quit eating so much of our good bread, it seemed like it had been a long time since you had last been here."

"Monique wants to go to a fancy shop to have her hair cut."

"You're going to let her cut her hair?" Madame Giroux cried out with alarm.

"I think it will be quite beautiful," Madame Reynaud replied, defending her daughter. "When she was little and her hair was shorter, she had beautiful soft dark curls. Besides, it is time she had what she wanted. She is nearly thirty."

"That is how it started with our daughter. You saw for yourself and know what heartbreak we had. First it was her hair, then she pierced her ears as though she came from Gypsies: short hair, pierced ears, short skirts followed by late nights and who knows what else before she got pregnant, married Philippe and finally settled down."

"The haircut was my idea," Madame Reynaud did not want to hear about Madame Giroux's simple daughter. "I thought it might lift her spirits. You know, she is not always well, and the mistral, well, she cannot even go out of the house for her walks around the neighborhood when the mistral is blowing."

"What a shame for one so sweet. That is always the way, is it not?"

"It is just the way it is. A good haircut from a fancy shop might be precisely what she needs to lift her spirits and give her the courage to get out a little more often."

"You are right. It is not good to be so confined."

"But, as you know, those new shops in town, the ones where everyone looks like they have just stepped out of a fancy lady magazine, can be unfriendly places."

"The women in those shops are terrible. Sometimes they come here for a loaf of bread, and on their way out the door they tell their friends that it is a shame they can't get good bread in Avignon. They are worse than the Parisians!"

"I knew you would understand. That is why I wish to borrow your fur coat this afternoon, so Monique might wear it to ward off their chill."

"A fine fur coat, like the one Monsieur Giroux so generously gave me, is just the thing to keep one warm in such a chilly place. I find it also helps in getting the attention of shop girls when one is in a hurry."

"So Monique may borrow your fine fur coat?"

"It would be my pleasure."

"Au revoir, Madame," Madame Reynaud said as she turned to leave.

"Au revoir, Madame," Madame Giroux called back, "and be sure to buy enough bread today from Monsieur Boffard so you and Monique will not starve!"

As quickly as Madame Reynaud could, because she could hear the wind whooping and gathering speed with each whoosh and twirl it made as it tried to rip the stubborn leaves from every bush and tree it touched, she tried to finish Madame Fleury's shopping. She dug down deep into the box for the softest prunes, got the cheese Madame Fleury wanted, and paid for the bananas. Then she carefully put the remaining money from the handkerchief into her coat pocket instead of her purse, so she could put the two croissants she had bought from Madame Giroux in her purse to keep them hidden from Monsieur Boffard.

When she stepped into Monsieur Boffard's tiny shop, she was relieved to see it was full of people. She did not want to get caught in a conversation with him again.

As soon as she pushed open his door, however, the crowd of people suddenly left just like the wind.

"Two baguettes," she ordered before he could ask her.

"Bonjour, Madame Reynaud," Monsieur Boffard said, straightening his back and pressing the front of his apron smooth with his hands. "Welcome to my humble shop."

"Two baguettes," she repeated, fumbling in her pocket for Madame Fleury's money, and the coins she needed to pay for her own baguette.

"Two baguettes," he said playfully, wrapping each around the middle in a short sheet of paper. "One for Madame Fleury, and one for you, Madame Reynaud."

"And a croissant."

"I am sorry," he said, pausing to look over Madame Reynaud's shoulder to see if anyone else was coming into the shop. "I cannot sell you a croissant."

"But you have a case full of croissants!"

"I know, but they are for others, not for you."

"For whom?"

"Those that do not know."

"Do not know what?" Madame Reynaud demanded, getting tired and angry and all the more determined than ever that he should sell her the croissant, for she surely could not go back to Madame Giroux with two stiff loaves of Monsieur Boffard's bread tucked beneath her arm.

"My croissants used to be good," he added sullenly. "These are not good. The weather was bad last night. The wind howled and spoiled the dough. These croissants are tough."

"I do not care," she said, extending her hand as though she were demanding a forbidden object be handed over instantly.

"Ah, but, you see, I care," he said.

Madame Reynaud was getting a little impatient with all his sudden caring.

"It is not for me," she said sharply as if she were speaking to an unruly child. "Madame Fleury wouldn't know a good croissant from a rock."

"Madame Fleury has been my faithful customer for years. She is an old woman, and not well. Had I known it was for her, I would not have even entertained the thought of selling you the croissant."

"So, you did consider selling it to me!" Madame Reynaud all but shouted, counting out six of the francs to pay for the two loaves of bread. "What good fortune it is for poor Madame Fleury that your shop is empty. If it had been full, perhaps you would have been less considerate of her age, and the possibility that a sharp edge of one of your tough croissants would have cut away yet another one of her teeth."

Then before he could respond, Madame Reynaud slapped the money on the counter, grabbed the two loves of bread, and headed out into the wind.

"Bonne journée," the big man laughed. "Bonne journée, Madame Reynaud, a bientôt!"

A GARDEN WALL IN PROVENCE

Before Madame Reynaud knocked on Madame Fleury's door to give her the groceries, she took the bag with the two croissants from Guy Giroux's out of her purse. "Madame Fleury," she called as she knocked.

"Ah, my dear Madame Reynaud," the old woman greeted her as she opened her door. She had dressed, but had put her old bathrobe on over her other clothes. "Oh," she said clasping her hands together when she saw the bag with the croissants in Madame Reynaud's extended hand. "TWO croissants. First you go out in this terrible weather to fetch my groceries, and now, a gift! Madame Reynaud, I am a lucky woman to have one so kind as you for my neighbor. Thank you!"

"You are more than welcome," Madame Reynaud sighed as she handed over the bag with the croissants, realizing they had cost her much more than she had intended. They had, however, bought her the use of Madame Giroux's coat, for which she was grateful.

"They are so big and soft! Monsieur Boffard seems to have outdone himself this morning!"

"Yes," Madame Reynaud said handing over the small bag of groceries and the cold baguette. "Monsieur Boffard has truly outdone himself."

Madame Reynaud apologized to Monique that they would once again be eating Monsieur Boffard's hard bread and would not have a soft sweet croissant from Guy Giroux's.

"I will say, however," she offered as she opened their two jars of jam and placed them on the breakfast table, "that we have Madame Fleury's desire for croissants to thank for the use of Madame Giroux's best fur coat."

"Why do we need her coat?"

"For your haircut."

"Since when does one need a fur coat in order to get a haircut?"

"Since one young lady I know decided she wanted to look like a magazine model."

"I don't want to look like a model. I just want my hair to look like the model's."

"It is the same," Madame Reynaud stiffened her back a little as she cut a chunk of baguette for herself and began to spread it with jam. "Besides, it is cold and you need to be warm."

"My own coat will keep me plenty warm."

"Not warm enough." Madame Reynaud said emphatically, signaling that the discussion about the coat was ended.

Monique took the knife to cut a slice of bread. "I would like," she said cautiously, "to go alone this afternoon."

"You are certainly old enough," Madame Reynaud said, her voice small and hurt.

"I would be pleased to wear the coat," Monique added.

"It is the perfect coat to keep away the chill."

THURSDAY AFTERNOON

"And, you let her go by herself, just like that?" Madame Pécaut said, stirring the second lump of sugar into her tea.

"Just like that," Madame Reynaud shrugged her shoulders and shook her head a little as though she hardly believed it herself. "She had tied her long hair together in a pony tail with a scarf so the wind wouldn't blow it every which way when she got out of the cab. She looked so pretty in Madame Giroux's coat with that silky knot of hair falling down across her left shoulder. Just like a model."

"Oui," Madame Pécaut nodded as though she had seen her too and had agreed. "She's not our little girl any more, is she?"

"She'll always be my little girl," Madame Reynaud resolved, adding another lump of sugar to her tea.

"Oui," Madame Pécaut agreed. Pantagruel whimpered a little in his sleep, his legs twitching and skittering on the polished wooden floor as though he were running in his dreams. "He's chasing rabbits," Madame Pécaut offered. "Even my little Charme dreamed of such things."

Pantagruel settled down, stretching his stout body until his hairy hide spread out like a thick rug on the floor in front of the kitchen door.

"I have never seen such a big dog," Madame Reynaud said in wonder.

"They told me his father weighed 70 kilos," Madame Pécaut said.

"Seventy kilos, oh-la-la!" Madame Reynaud responded, shaking the open palm of her hand.

"Monsieur Pécaut did not weigh so much," Madame Pécaut sighed.

"He was little, but strong. A handsome man," Madame Reynaud added out of respect for Madame Pécaut's deceased husband.

"Thank you."

The two women sat in silence watching Pantagruel twitch and stretch as he filled the doorway of the room and dreamed of chasing rabbits.

"Seventy kilos," Madame Reynaud shook her head.

"A big dog," Madame Pécaut agreed.

Pantagruel shivered, and his thick coat rippled like a wave down his body. He shook his head, snorting a little through his nose before he curled himself up again for sleep.

"Too big for a snake to eat."

Madame Pécaut took a sip from her cup and nodded her head as she looked at the sleeping dog. "Unless it is a very big snake."

"A snake that big would be too big to be carried home from the university in a pillow case."

"It is a good thing Monsieur Duncan does not have a car."

"A very good thing," Madame Reynaud agreed as she watched the sleeping dog begin to twitch and dream again of chasing rabbits.

"It is not my coat," Monique told the tall thin man who had taken the heavy fur coat from her shoulders when she stepped into the beautiful shop. He stood by her side and waited patiently as she used her cane to make her way to the chair where he would cut her hair.

"It is not my shop," he smiled, offering his arm to help her to his chair. "So we are even."

"Even?"

"All the ladies who come into our shop wearing their fine fur coats want their hair cut by the famous Jean Pierre Louis. This is his shop, but he is never here. He lives in Paris and cuts hair there. So, when they come in and see me, they assume I am Jean Pierre because I am the only man who works here. So, they make their appointments with me. But, I am not Jean Pierre. I know they think I am, and the girls who work here know they think I am, so we don't say anything. We let them assume I am Jean Pierre Louis, and they always leave happy."

"Why don't you tell them?"

"Have you ever tried to tell a lady who wears a fur coat anything?"

"But you told me."

"It is not your coat."

"But you only know it isn't my coat because I told you it wasn't my coat."

"You wear the coat as though you are afraid it might come to life and bite you. But a lady who owns a fur coat wears it in such a way as to let the world know that she is the one that bites."

Monique laughed, "Madame Giroux can be a difficult woman."

"I have no doubt. It is an exceptionally fine coat."

"It was my mother's idea."

"Not a bad idea, just one that doesn't fit you well."

Monique looked around for a moment to let her mind gather in everything she saw in the shop: the white tiled floors, white leather chairs, big clear unframed mirrors hanging from the ceiling as though they were polished silver clouds, and the barely audible sound of classical music radiating mysteriously from the walls.

"If you find the music annoying, I'll have Lydia turn it up or off. There is no one else here this afternoon so I doubt it would matter. Jean Pierre believes playing music so softly as almost not to be able to hear it is soothing. Some of our customers find it to be more like the buzzing of bees than something soothing. Others are so busy chattering on about their important lives, they don't even notice it is playing."

"It is quite soothing," Monique said, closing her eyes.

"Can you hear better with your eyes closed?"

"I do not go to very many fancy places," Monique offered, nodding toward her cane. "If I look around, then close my eyes, I can force my mind to make a picture of what I see so I can take it home with me."

"You don't need the coat."

"But, I need the cane."

"You carry each other well."

"Thank you."

"So," he said, untying the scarf from around her pony tail and taking the long length of her dark silken hair in his hands, letting it fall down across her shoulders and back. "What would you like me to do with this lovely hair of yours?"

"Cut it off," Monique said, reaching into the pocket of her skirt for the picture she had torn from the magazine.

"It is none of my business, but have you and your lover had a quarrel?"

"A quarrel?"

"Quarrels between lovers often seem to end in hair cuts. I once made the mistake of cutting someone's hair that was thick and beautiful like yours. It looked as if scissors had never touched it. I was foolishly flattered the woman had come to me to have her hair cut, but I learned only too soon that she had just had a fight with her lover. He came storming into the shop, and I would have had my nose broken if the woman had not gotten out of her chair and pulled him off of me. So, you see, if there has been a quarrel, I cannot cut your hair."

"I have no lover."

"Well, then we're in business, as the Americans say."

"And I want it cut like this," Monique opened the folded magazine picture and spread it out in her lap.

"Ah, so you are looking for a bold transformation."

"Sunday's my birthday, my thirtieth birthday."

"Then it is time for a change."

"Can you do this?" Monique asked holding up the picture.

"I have already confessed that I am not the famous Jean Pierre Louis, but," he said pointing with the tip of his scissors at the picture, "I can do this if. . ."

"If what?"

"If you let me take you out for an aperitif at six on Sunday."

"Without the coat?"

"Without the coat."

FRIDAY MORNING

Madame Reynaud was about to tell Monique about the fête she had planned for her birthday on Sunday when Madame Pécaut screamed. It was a scream so loud and so high, it threw open the shutters of a half dozen of the little houses lining their alleyway.

"Stop him!" Madame Pécaut shouted, grabbing a broom and running at her fence, aiming to hit Monsieur Duncan before he could throw something over the fence to Pantagruel. "He is trying to poison my dog. Help!"

Pantagruel was alternately barking and anxiously watching both Madame Pécaut and Monsieur Duncan, trying to determine if it was safe to take what Monsieur Duncan had in his hand, or if he did, would he be the one hit on the snout with the upraised broom.

Just as Monsieur Duncan covered his head in order to protect himself from the oncoming blows of Madame Pécaut's broom, Pantagruel saw his chance to snatch the crust of bread in Monsieur Duncan's outstretched hand. But Monsieur Duncan's hand was now too high in the air for the dog to safely reach it without jumping. When Pantagruel leaped for the bread, he missed and crashed into Madame Pécaut, knocking her to the ground.

"Help, somebody, help, the dog is attacking me," Madame Pécaut screamed.

"Don't move," Madame Fleury shouted from her bedroom window, "I've called the police. Don't move, either one of you!"

Pantagruel threw himself on top of Madame Pécaut's sprawled out body in an attempt to protect her from whatever danger Madame Fleury was shouting about. The dog, teeth bared, eyes riveted on Monsieur Duncan and the piece of bread still in his outstretched hand, began to snarl.

"The dog is too big for you," Monsieur Duncan said calmly, never taking his eyes from the snarling dog, while being careful not to make any sudden moves with the bread in his hand.

"Who do you think you are?" Madame Pécaut snapped back, trying to push Pantagruel away from her face. "Telling me how big my dog should be!"

"You shouldn't keep him out in the yard at night. He wants to sleep inside in order to protect you. By putting him outside, he thinks he has to patrol your yard in order to make sure you are safe. That's why he barked so much last night, and why your flowers are all trampled."

Madame Pécaut let her eyes drop to the edge of her yard where she saw, for the first time, that Pantagruel had walked a neat path along the edge of her garden walls destroying her flower beds.

"They tend sheep," Monsieur Duncan explained.

"Who does?"

"Great Pyrenees. That's the only thing they know how to do. It doesn't matter to the dog that there are no sheep in your garden. All he knows is you put him out there last night, and if he was put out there, as far as he is concerned, he was there to tend sheep, or to take care of something, so he did the only thing he knew how to do, he walked the edge of your garden making sure everything was safe."

Madame Pécaut could not speak. She could only stare at the path of destruction Pantagruel had managed in just one short night. Where once had been plants, there was now a trampled path of slick viridian green, as though an artist had laid a thick stripe of paint around the edge of her property with a palate knife.

"If you let the dog sleep inside at night, he will spend the night quietly on the floor guarding your house. And don't bother with a bed or even a blanket. He doesn't want it. He prefers the stone floor, the cooler the better."

"How could you know what my dog wants?"

"Don't speak to him," Madame Fleury screeched from the perch of her second story window. "The police are coming!"

Not wanting the police to see her lying on the ground covered by a dog, Madame Pécaut tried to get up, but as she pushed the heavy furry hide of Pantagruel, he didn't budge. Instead, he began to growl a low dangerous kind of growl that made Madame Pécaut slowly pull her hands away and be still.

"Easy," Monsieur Duncan cooed. "Easy there big guy. He's confused," he continued in the same cooing manner talking to Madame Pécaut, his voice even and soft, his hand still outstretched and unmoving, his eyes on the dog. "You must move carefully and talk to him softly, let him know you are safe. He can't figure out what is happening. It is very confusing to him with Madame Fleury shouting at us that the police are coming and me standing here offering him a piece of bread. He's a puppy. He'll get it straight in a little while, but right now, he's a puppy and he's in a strange place with new people, and he's been working all night long trying to protect his new home, and now he's trying to protect you and you must reassure him you are safe. When you talk to the police, be calm. Do not scream or raise your voice. Madame Reynaud," Monsieur Duncan lifted his head a little in order to let Madame Reynaud know he was talking to her, "Bring the police into your yard so they can see from over your fence what is going on, and tell them to please not shout. Everything is fine."

Madame Reynaud did not bother to ask Madame Pécaut's approval, but instead, ran to her garden gate in order to stop the police before they could get to Madame Pécaut's garden. When she returned, with two police officers in tow, Madame Pécaut was sitting up stroking Pantagruel's big bear-like head and talking softly to Monsieur Duncan. Just as things began to quiet down, Monsieur Duncan raised his hand and tossed the hunk of bread into the air to Pantagruel. The dog caught it without having to leave Madame Pécaut's side.

"Stop him!" Madame Fleury screamed from her window perch. "He's trying to poison the dog!"

Pantagruel's large white ears shot back flat against his head, and the fur ruffled around his collar. Madame Pécaut froze, her hand firm on the dog's broad back, and spoke to her neighbor without turning her head. "Stop screeching like a wounded bird Madame Fleury and get into your house. It's only a piece of bread."

"The man's the Devil," the old woman shouted to the police officers. "He keeps snakes in his house. I have seen them myself. Snakes big enough to eat a dog in one bite."

"You must forgive her," Madame Pécaut smiled to the officers. "She is old and doesn't eat well."

"I tell you, he is trying to poison her dog!" Madame Fleury shouted.

The two officers looked at each other, then at Madame Fleury who was not shouting any longer, but pointing instead, as though her silent condemnation of Monsieur Duncan was proof enough of his guilt.

"Could you tell us what happened here?" the shorter officer asked Madame Pécaut.

"He was only giving him a piece of bread, Madame Reynaud saw so herself, and in the excitement, the dog, who is but a puppy and does not know any better, knocked me down."

"Yes?" the other officer questioned Madame Reynaud as though he wished it were so, so they could go back to the station. He had no desire to investigate anything to do with snakes.

Madame Reynaud looked first at her neighbor, Madame Fleury, who was still perched at her open window, then at Madame Pécaut who was now playfully rubbing the thick white fur on Pantagruel's back. Madame Reynaud did not wish to cross Madame Fleury, nor disagree with Madame Pécaut. But, if Madame Pécaut, who was the one to first claim Monsieur Duncan was trying to poison her dog, now said he was only trying to give him a piece of bread, she believed it must be so.

"Madame Fleury meant well, but her eyes are bad," Madame Reynaud said softly, hoping Madame Fleury could not hear. "As you can see, the dog is quite happy. If the bread was poisoned, wouldn't the dog be dead by now?"

"These things can take time," the shorter officer offered.

"No, you are wrong," the second one said, shaking his head at what his partner was saying. "If it were poison, I know for a fact, the dog would be dead. If it were a bigger dog perhaps, one that was full grown, it could take some time. But this, as she has pointed out, is but a puppy. And a puppy, well, a puppy would be dead by now."

"But he is a big dog," the other officer said.

"I tell you, the man is a Devil!" Madame Fleury shouted from her window. "He keeps snakes. You must see for yourself and then you will know I am telling the truth."

"A puppy," the other officer insisted shaking his head.

"You are probably right," the shorter officer agreed, hoping by agreeing that the matter could now be settled, and they could be on their way.

"The constant whistling of the mistral in the middle of the night has made Madame Fleury a bit crazy," Madame Pécaut said, idly scratching Pantagruel behind the ears.

"So, it was just bread?" the shorter officer asked Monsieur Duncan.

"Puppies like bread," Monsieur Duncan replied.

"Toasted?" the officer asked.

"I hadn't thought about toasting the bread," Monsieur Duncan said.

"Mine will only eat it toasted. Day-old and toasted. Dry as a bone, you know."

"I'll have to try that."

"Everything is fine, Madame," the officer called up to Madame Fleury. "The puppy is fine."

"You haven't found the snake. You've got to look for the snake," she called back, her finger fanning the air in warning.

"I am a biology professor at the University," Monsieur Duncan offered. "It is true, I once brought home a snake. A sick snake. But he is well now and back at the University in my lab."

"Then there is no snake now," the second officer spoke loudly so Madame Pécaut would be sure to hear.

"Not anymore," Monsieur Duncan affirmed.

"The snake is gone," the officer called up to Madame Fleury, waving his hands in front of him to emphasize the meaning of gone.

Madame Fleury closed the shutters of her house with a clatter and a bang.

Madame Reynaud did not question Madame Pécaut's wisdom in the matter with the dog. As she had observed herself, Monsieur Duncan did seem to know a great deal about big dogs and it was clear now, since the dog was neither dead nor sick, that what he had offered Pantagruel was only a piece of stale bread.

"So," Monique asked anxiously once the ordeal was over, "Whose dog is it now?"

"I guess," Madame Reynaud continued, struggling to cut through one of Monsieur Boffard's crusty baguettes, buttering it both top and bottom in order to soften it and make it more palatable, "it is all of ours. Without question, it was our four cases of wine that paid for him. Since it is Madame Pécaut's dog, she will feed him and keep him in her house at night. And, because the dog is really too big for either one of us to take him out on a leash, it will be Monsieur Duncan who will take him for walks."

"Incredible!" Monique laughed.

Monique had been meaning to ask her mother all week about the four cartons of wine now stashed under their stairwell in the hallway. But the excitement of Pantagruel's arrival and her own adventure of getting a haircut had kept their quiet household in a flutter.

"She was quite a sight lying there with that big dog covering her skinny body like one of grandmother's big goose feather quilts," Monique added.

"I believe it will be best if we forget Madame Pécaut was ever on the ground covered with our dog."

"The walls are thin," Monique agreed.

"I'm afraid we have a little mending to do on the wall with Madame Fleury. However, she should not be too angry with us since she is again eating her beloved bread from Monsieur Boffard's. And, as recompense, we are taking her with us to the Fête at St. Joseph's tonight."

"Oh yes," Monique had almost forgotten, "Monsieur Boffard's gâteau des rois and the Fête for the Three Kings."

FRIDAY EVENING

Everyone in St. Joseph's parish always showed up for cake and champagne at the Fête of the Three Kings, which made Father Didier want to deliver a sermon about the faithful. However, the vestry wouldn't allow it, saying it was important for the congregation to enjoy a little fellowship. It was also important for them to sell a lot of tickets.

Fellowship was one of those things Father Didier detested about the "new" church. It seemed to him that fellowship was what got most good Catholics into trouble.

If he had been allowed to speak, he thought it would be best to start with the story of the Three Kings. He doubted many of the people now crowding through the door of the church gymnasium, in order to drink champagne and eat cake in the hopes of finding a silly little china figurine and be crowned king, could correctly identify one of the Three Kings if they came, camel in tow, down center court and shot one of their gifts through a basket.

Basketball was another thing that got on Father Didier's nerves. The very same vestry that wouldn't let him speak at the Fête had shown similar bad judgment when they voted to build a gymnasium with basketball hoops instead of a new baptism font. When Father Didier questioned their decision to put a basketball court in the gym, there came a united outcry from the vestry (the only time the vestry had EVER been united that Father Didier could remember) that there was no other place for kids to play basketball in St. Joseph's Parish, while they had a perfectly good baptistery already.

Father Didier had wondered if any kids in St. Joseph even knew how to play basketball. He couldn't understand what he had ever done so wrong to be punished by being sent to such a ridiculous parish.

"So many people," Monsieur Boffard beamed, grabbing the priest by the hand and giving it a sound shaking.

"Yes," Father Didier answered, trying to move out of the big man's range and hoping he wouldn't feel obliged to greet him with the required three kisses of Avignon: another silly thing about this place that got on his nerves. How he wished he were back in Paris!

"Who would have thought so many people would come to eat my cake?"

"They always come for the cake and the champagne," answered Father Didier.

"But, this year, they come for my cake."

"Yes," Father Didier agreed, knowing there was no other course of conversation worth pursuing with this simple man.

"I would be pleased, given the large turnout, to offer my fine cakes to the Church for next year. It is the least I can do."

"You'll have to speak to the vestry."

"A wonderful idea," Monsieur Boffard crowed, pumping the small man's hand again as though he were trying to raise the rear end of a car with a jack. "I'll speak to the vestry."

At that moment, Monsieur Boffard saw Madame Reynaud standing alone under the home team's basket and stopped pumping Father

Didier's hand.

"Madame Reynaud," he bellowed, moving across the room. "Bonsoir. And welcome to my fête."

"Bonsoir, Monsieur Boffard," she nodded cordially.

"That is a beautiful dress you have on this evening."

"It is old."

"Old can be beautiful," he said, squeezing her hand a little as he greeted her.

"Are you saying I am old?"

"I am saying you are beautiful and I am quite taken with you."

"Oh, Monsieur Boffard," Madame Reynaud said. She had not wanted to, but she was blushing and she could now feel the heat rise from her shoulders to her cheeks. Champagne always made her blush. She knew she had made a mistake to drink the first glass then take another so quickly, but Madame Fleury had gotten on her nerves with her incessant squawking about Monsieur Duncan's snake and Madame Pécaut's dog, she had no choice but to drink the second to calm herself. Thank heavens Monique was there and was able to steer Madame Fleury over to the table with the cakes and away from her for a few moments so she could have her third glass of champagne in peace.

"You look good with a little color in your cheeks!" Monsieur Boffard said, noting that the choice of his words had brought even more color to her face. "I have always thought champagne made women more beautiful, don't you agree?"

By now, her cheeks were burning. To argue with him would only make them burn hotter and longer.

"A piece of cake?" Monsieur Boffard asked, offering her his

outstretched arm.

"Of course," she answered, placing her hand on his arm in hopes of regaining her balance. It had been so long since she had drunk champagne, she had forgotten how it bubbled straight to her head and made her legs feel wobbly. A piece of cake might be just the thing to help her sober up a little.

"What are you hoping to find this year?" Madame Fleury asked Monique as she poked and prodded her piece of cake with her thin fingers, carefully pulling up both the candied pineapple slice and the cherry to be sure they weren't hiding a little figurine before she took her first cautious bite.

"Another angel would be nice, but I'd take a shepherd or even a king."

"I once lost a tooth on a shepherd."

"I remember. An ambulance brought you home," Monique said.

"I thought I had swallowed the little man."

"I think someone later found him under your chair."

"Father Didier told me Monsieur Duprés found him. He never gave him back."

"Monsieur Duprés has a whole collection of santons and a splendid crèche he keeps in his office at school. If you were sick, and you had to go to his office to rest, you could play with them."

"It was my shepherd," Madame Fleury announced.

"He says the children are always finding the santons in their cakes, then losing them in the excitement."

"It was mine."

Monique looked around the gym for her mother.

"It's good cake this year, don't you think?" Monique asked.

"A little dry," Madame Fleury answered. "It's always a little dry. That's why they have to serve champagne."

"I never thought about it like that before," Monique said, happy to have left the topic of the little lost shepherd behind.

"Nothing," the old woman exclaimed, her finger was poked clear through the cake like a sword. "Could you get me another piece of cake?" she asked Monique as she sucked a tiny morsel of pineapple from the tips of her fingers, wrapping the last torn bit of cake in her napkin and stuffing it into her purse.

Happy to have a reason to get away from Madame Fleury, Monique stood up from the table. When she turned around to get her cane from the back of her chair, she saw her mother and Monsieur Boffard walking arm-in-arm out of the gym.

"I want to tell you something you probably already know," Monsieur Boffard said, his voice almost a whisper in the cool air of the evening. "I must tell you so I don't have to think about it anymore."

Madame Reynaud was not sure she wanted to know anything more about Monsieur Boffard than she did already. However, she was unable to stop him because her whole body was spinning with champagne and the sweet taste of cake. Her head was quite fuzzy, and her tongue felt numb. The champagne was making it difficult for her to speak, so she let her chin drop in a nod, hoping Monsieur Boffard would continue to stand still and let her hold on to his arm so she would not fall down.

"It is not my bread."

"What?" Madame Reynaud said, trying not to shout.

"At my shop. It is not my bread."

Madame Reynaud could not respond because the "What?" she had inadvertently shouted was now rattling menacingly through her body. She clung helplessly to the thick arm of Monsieur Boffard, hoping she wouldn't pass out and fall down.

"When my wife was alive we used to get up together in the middle of the night and go downstairs to start the ovens. We were like kids sneaking down for Christmas. Around six, when the first batch of baguettes went into the oven, and the smell of yeast and baked bread had warmed the shop, she would make coffee. Together we would eat the prettiest loaf of the batch while it was still hot, spreading it with marmalade and butter. That's how she liked her bread, fresh from the oven with orange marmalade and butter."

He stopped talking for a moment, putting his hand over Madame Reynaud's hand that was now firmly embedded in his arm.

"After she died. I had to force myself to get up and go down to start the ovens alone. 'You're old,' I told myself, 'too old to learn how to do something else.'" Monsieur Boffard stopped, waiting for Madame Reynaud to laugh at his little joke, but she stood still, her warm hand still on his arm. "I felt like I was going to go crazy getting up night after night alone. Then I heard about a factory where you could get bread that was already made and shaped into loaves, ready for you to bake. If I used this bread, all I would have to do would be to turn on the ovens and bake the bread. It would be easier, different than it was when my precious Muriel was alive and could help me."

He paused again, hoping Madame Reynaud might say something, but she stood firm, her shaking fingers digging into his arm.

"The man who drives the truck understands my secret, and he comes in the middle of the night when no one can see him. He has a key. When I go down at five-thirty, the bread is sitting on the tables waiting for me, ready to be baked. They are not my croissants, either."

As Monsieur Boffard's little speech had unwound itself, his large warm body moving closer to hers as he spoke, Madame Reynaud felt the parking lot begin to spin.

When Madame Reynaud's knees buckled a little, causing her to hold onto him ever more tightly, Monsieur Boffard mistook the effects of the champagne to be a willingness on her part to befriend him. So he took her in his arms and kissed her.

SATURDAY MORNING

Madame Reynaud envied people who woke up the next morning and could not remember what had happened. Unfortunately, she remembered everything. Monsieur Boffard kissing her. Father Didier coming out to the parking lot to smoke a cigarette and catching them kissing. Madame Fleury accusing Monsieur Duprés of having stolen her shepherd. Monsieur Boffard furiously cutting up a half dozen of the gâteaux des rois in the hopes of finding another shepherd in order to quiet the hysterical Madame Fleury. Madame Pécaut struggling with Pantagruel in order to keep him from eating the cake off the tables, as well as from eating the little toy poodle Madame Duprés carried with her everywhere in her purse.

And then, the last terrible scene, when Monsieur Boffard found a shepherd and raised it high over his head in triumph and Pantagruel, mistaking the gesture, leaped at his hand to snatch the morsel of cake still clinging to the small shepherd, knocking Monsieur Boffard onto the refreshment table, which then collapsed causing an explosion of popping corks and a flood of champagne across the gym floor.

Then, when Madame Reynaud, Monique, Madame Pécaut, Madame Fleury, and Pantagruel came home together in a taxi, the driver insisting they sit on newspapers so their wet clothes would not stain the upholstery in his car. By the time they reached the Impasse de l'Alliance, news of Marseilles beating Milan in the first round of the Coupe d'Europe was smudged across the rear end of Madame Reynaud's dress, and the front of her dress was soaked through with drool.

Although Pantagruel seemed content to stay seated on the floor of the taxi, neatly covering their feet, the dog insisted, despite her gentle nudging, on resting his head in Madame Reynaud's lap all the way home.

None of this would have been so bad if it hadn't been for Monsieur Boffard: Monsieur Boffard kissing her, Monsieur Boffard searching for the shepherd in order to quiet Madame Fleury, Monsieur Boffard laughing that big terrible laugh of his while the champagne spread over the floor and Father Didier flew into a rage. Then later, Monsieur Boffard begging to please let him take them home, stuffing money into the taxi driver's shirt pocket so they would not have to pay.

Madame Reynaud lay in bed listening to Monique put on the kettle for tea. Earlier she had heard Monique make her way down the stairs, her cane banging against the railing at each step as she moved her hand in order to help her descend.

Madame Reynaud's head was still spinning from last night's champagne, and she thought better of trying to get out of bed to go help her daughter. Instead, she lay in bed, counting the stairs as Monique took them one at a time. Halfway down, stair seven, Monique stopped. Madame Reynaud had assumed she needed to rest, but, when she heard the ratcheting flip of the front door chime, she knew Monique was waiting to hear the whistle and call of the postman signaling he had left a package for them hanging from their box. Instead, they both heard the heavy footsteps of a man walking down their street.

A few minutes later Monique called out from the foot of the stairs:

"The tea is ready."

"Not this morning," Madame Reynaud called back, searching for the fringe of the chenille spread, hoping she could find it and pull it up over her head and go back to sleep.

"Yes, this morning," Monique called back, insisting she come. "Besides, there is a present waiting for you, and it is still warm."

Madame Reynaud grabbed her robe and nearly flew down the stairs. The footsteps they had heard had been Monsieur Boffard's.

"Mon Dieu," Madame Reynaud gasped, drawing her robe tight against her body. "What is it?"

"I believe," Monique said, lifting one flap of the huge cardboard box now blocking the hallway, "it is a freshly baked gâteau des rois."

Monique watched her mother's face while Madame Reynaud cautiously lifted the other flap of the box.

"It is a very large gâteau des rois," Monique said.

"From Monsieur Boffard," Madame Reynaud offered.

Madame Reynaud hoped the admission would be enough to answer whatever questions Monique had about last night.

"Yes," Monique confirmed.

The two women stood in silence looking down at the large halo shaped cake. The sweet smell, once the top of the box was open and the cake was cooling, filled their little hallway.

"If we work together, I believe we can lift it out of the box and onto the table," Monique said, bending down to slip her hands under the gâteau as she spoke. "We don't want to break it."

The two of them, Madame Reynaud holding on with two hands, Monique balancing her end in one hand as she used her cane in the other to steady her walk, slipped the cake from its box and carried it successfully to their dining room table. The tea cart was already there, a pot of hot tea sitting on a trivet, a fresh lemon sliced on a plate, as well as cups and saucers, plates, silverware and napkins ready at their places.

"Don't you think we should cut the cake?" Monique said with obvious glee.

"For breakfast?" Madame Reynaud asked, not knowing what they should do with this thing that had earlier blocked their hallway and now nearly filled their small dining table.

"Why not?"

"Yes, why not?"

Monique handed her mother the knife. Madame Reynaud took a long hard look at the immense round cake. She had never seen anything quite so tempting. After careful consideration, she selected a section marked neatly with two bright yellow slices of pineapple and a plump red cherry, and began to cut the first piece.

"A santon!" she cried out as the edge of her knife touched a tiny china figurine. She moved the knife over a few centimeters and began cutting again. "And another!"

Monique took the knife from her mother's shaking hand and with the point began probing the cake from side to side.

"The cake is full of santons!"

Madame Reynaud reached for the gâteau and tore a chunk from it. As her fingers searched through the warm soft dough she called out the names of the figures as she pulled them free and placed them on her plate.

"The surprised peasant, the napping shepherd, a lamb, the first wise man, a camel, the baby Jesus, an angel!"

She and her mother tasted little bits here and there of the cake as they explored for santons. They both felt the cake was much sweeter and tenderer than the one they had had last night. However, after awhile, eating the cake seemed less important than finding all the figurines, so they let the crumbs fall on the table and roll out onto the floor as their fingers tore through the gâteau.

Once they had eaten as much of the cake and drunk as much tea as either of them could hold, Monique gathered up all the santons they had found in Monsieur Boffard's magnificent cake and took them into the kitchen to wash them. When the santons were all washed and dried, she arranged them on the buffet. There were thirty-seven in total, all different, except the three tiny piglets Monique had carefully placed together with the mother pig, so they might, if they sprang to life, nurse. There had also been three camels, one for each Wise Man, but if you looked closely, you could see they were different: one had a blue blanket thrown on his back, another red with a small touch of yellow at each of the corners as if there were golden tassels hanging from it, and the third had no blanket at all.

It was a totally wonderful and foolish thing: an entire village baked into one gigantic cake.

After she had swept up the crumbs, Madame Reynaud left the house in order to take their ruined dresses from the night before to the laundry. The Gypsies were there, their dirty clothes stacked like great anthills all around the room, while a dozen or so machines spun and churned.

One of the big dryers buzzed. The sound shook through Madame

Reynaud's tired body. The combination of three glasses of champagne last night along with one too many slices of sweet cake with her morning tea had left her senses a little jangled.

In addition, the heat of the laundry and the smell from the big dry cleaning machine, where their dresses from last night were now splashing and spinning in their chemical stew had made her head so dizzy Madame Reynaud had to sit down on one of the plastic chairs bolted to the floor. Had they not been fastened to the floor, she would have chosen to take one of them outside and sit in the cool fresh air of the morning while the machine did its work.

She did not like being in the laundry when the Gypsies were there. The two Gypsy men, the old one who always slept in his chair and the young one who drank so much, left right as she came in, leaving only the old Gypsy woman to stuff all their laundry into the big machines. Madame Reynaud was glad the men did not stay because the sour smell of the one who drank too much would have been more than she could have handled this morning.

As it was, the Gypsy woman seemed to be agitated and kept pacing the room from the dryers to the washers, rubbing the large gold locket on the thick gold chain she always wore around her neck.

"Why are you so afraid?" the Gypsy suddenly shouted at Madame Reynaud, rushing towards her as though she wanted to hit her.

Madame Reynaud held onto the arms of the plastic chair.

"This man you are thinking about, the one who did something that scared you last night," the Gypsy woman hissed, "is a fool, but he loves you. You are old. You should be happy to take him into your bed."

"This is none of your business," Madame Reynaud shouted.

"Hush!" the Gypsy woman commanded. "I am telling you the truth. He is a kind man. Better than the drunken man I have, and besides, your daughter is going to leave you. If you turn your back now, you will be alone."

Madame Reynaud wanted to cover her ears to the Gypsy's words, but her hands held fast to the cold arms of the plastic chair.

"I don't believe you," Madame Reynaud said. "What do you know of my daughter?"

The Gypsy woman laughed, throwing her head back so the sound could roll up her throat and fill the room.

"And if I told you that your daughter will stay with you forever and you will suddenly be happy and rich, would you believe me then? Telling people what they want to hear is a trick all Gypsies use to make money."

The Gypsy stopped laughing and approached Madame Reynaud until she was standing so close in front of her, Madame Reynaud could smell the woody scent of a recent campfire on her hair. The Gypsy woman held the locket in her closed hand. When she came within inches of Madame Reynaud's face, she stretched out her hand as though she were offering Madame Reynaud a piece of chocolate or a precious jewel.

"But I have not asked you for money. And I am no ordinary Gypsy, for I have seen my only child die. I have held him in my arms as his soul left, and his body turned to stone."

The Gypsy woman opened her hand, and as she did, the locket opened. In it was a picture of a young child with dark thick curls and odd pale blue eyes. The small boy's eyes were neither laughing nor sober, but staring out from the locket as though he had been trapped there and was still alive and could see everything there was to see and know.

"He lives in my heart, and now, and with his innocent eyes, I can see what others cannot."

Then the Gypsy woman laughed again. It was a terrible laugh that drowned out the sound of the laundry machines and raced through Madame Reynaud's veins until the soft thudding of the champagne was gone, and the dangerous sound of the Gypsy's voice pounded through her head.

"It is the loneliness in the world that stirs the dead," the Gypsy said, snapping the locket closed. "You know the truth. Listen to your heart."

Before Madame Reynaud could ask her what else she knew, the Gypsy woman turned away from her and began to fold her laundry as though nothing had been said between the two of them.

Monique waited until she was sure her mother had made her way down their street, around the corner and into the laundry before she put on her coat and got her cane in order to walk to Monsieur Boffard's.

If Madame Pécaut would have had the good sense to leave Pantagruel home last night instead of insisting on taking him to the Fête to show him off, the evening might have ended differently. However, if it hadn't been for Pantagruel, Monsieur Boffard might have never been forced to be so forward with her mother as to bake the huge gâteau des rois.

Had Monique not seen, with her own eyes, her mother walking arm-in-arm with Monsieur Boffard, she would not have believed it was true. But she had. And now, it was clear to Monique, if there was ever going to be a reconciliation between her proud mother and Monsieur Boffard, she was going to have to make it happen.

The wind was cold and biting, but fresh in the way the mistral is always fresh, and the sky so clear and blue you would think, except for the cold and the occasional wind, it would be a perfect day for a picnic.

Monique straightened her shoulders and pushed her left hand deep into her coat pocket while she carried her cane in her right, steadying her walk as she went past the window of Guy Giroux's shop. She did not want Madame Giroux to suspect what she was up to, and felt it would be best if it just looked like she was going for a stroll.

As she approached Monsieur Boffard's shop she could see there were three customers waiting in line, so she walked to the end of the block and waited. She did not know exactly what she was going to say to Monsieur Boffard but thought it was best that whatever she had to say to him would be said in private.

When Monique thought enough time had passed for the other customers to make their choices and pay for their purchases, she walked back toward the shop. The wind was cold and pushed against her shoulders. Had she been a little boat, she would have sailed down the boulevard to the ramparts in one smooth stroke. In order to stay standing she had to plant her feet wide apart and place her cane firmly on the ground.

The three customers who had been in the shop came out one at a time, each carrying their long thin baguettes tucked under their arms in order to keep them from flying away. As the last one came out, Monique looked up and down the boulevard to make sure no one else was coming. When she put her hand to the handle of the door, it swung open with a sudden cold blast of wind.

"Bonjour, Mademoiselle Monique," Monsieur Boffard nodded his head and smiled.

"Bonjour, Monsieur Boffard."

"The cake," he started to say.

"Was wonderful."

"A silly thing."

"So many santons! A whole village of little saints!" Monique exclaimed.

"I wanted to apologize."

"My mother was wondering if you could come to our home for an aperitif."

"I would be honored," Monsieur Boffard said with a deep sweeping bow.

"Tomorrow, at six."

"I will be there!"

Madame Reynaud believed the Gypsy had put a spell on her, for when she left the laundry, her feet carried her down the Boulevard St. Ruf and into the shop of Monsieur Boffard.

"I would like you to come for aperitifs tomorrow evening at six," she announced without bothering to either greet him or wait for his greeting.

"I have heard, and again, I am honored."

"Then, you will come?"

"But, of course," he answered with a smile and a tip of his head.

"Good," Madame Reynaud added, wondering who had already told him of Monique's fête. "Tomorrow at six."

She left his shop and went to the florist to buy an armful of bright yellow mimosa branches and a big bouquet of crisp white baby's breath. When she got home, she was surprised to see their dresses, all clean, steam pressed and on hangers, dangling from the lip of their mailbox. With a start, she remembered she had left the laundry without ever taking their clothes from the machine.

SATURDAY AFTERNOON

Monique thought it had been a very strange day. First there was the giant gâteau des rois from Monsieur Boffard. Then, their dresses, cleaned and pressed, found hanging from their mailbox and, last, but surely not the least: the flowers.

For no apparent reason at all, her mother had bought flowers. As far as Monique could remember, the last time there had been flowers in their home was when her father was alive. Flowers were a part of life with him. Without fail, every Friday, he came home from work precisely at six with a bouquet of fresh flowers. Once the flowers were arranged in one of their many pretty vases, the three of them would sit down for tea with the good china.

It had been a wonderful little ritual, but it disappeared when he died. The good china was brought out now only for company and what her mother called affairs of the estate: those rare and formal occasions when Grandmother Reynaud took the train from Arles to come for Sunday supper.

But today, without any explanation, her mother had bought flowers and spent the whole afternoon arranging them in vases. First she put the mimosa and baby's breath she had purchased into their tallest crystal vase and placed them on the little walnut cabinet in the hallway. Once that was done, she left without saying a word and returned a half hour later carrying four more bundles of flowers: a dozen pale peach roses, a half dozen giant white calla lilies, a bunch of multi-colored freesia, and a dozen bright yellow jonquils.

She filled her grandmother's silver pitcher with the delicate roses and calla lilies. Once that was done, she went out into their yard and cut a dozen or more slender branches from their olive tree and made a daring arrangement of freesia and olive branches in a squat Waterford vase that had been a wedding present, and placed it in the center of their dining room buffet, all the while humming to herself and occasionally even singing.

Her mother was in such a strange mood, Monique did not know exactly how or when she was going to tell her about Monsieur Boffard coming for aperitifs on Sunday at six. Once, while her mother was stripping the bottom of the olive branches so she could place them in the arrangement with the freesia, Monique came into the kitchen hoping to talk with her about what she had done. Before she could say anything, her mother turned from her work and said: "Don't you just love freesia?"

To which Monique gave the only possible rational reply: "Yes."

Around four, Madame Reynaud put the kettle on for tea, then she got down the two stout blue vases they had bought from the glass blowers at Fontaine de Vaucluse and filled them with jonquils. She went upstairs and placed a vase of jonquils in each of their bedrooms and called out for Monique to come into the dining room to have tea.

"I've been thinking," Madame Reynaud said to Monique as she filled her daughter's cup, "that you should go talk to Valerie."

"Valerie?" Monique asked, as baffled by her mother's suggestion she talk with Valerie as she was by the appearance of Monsieur Boffard's gateau des rois this morning or the fresh flowers now adorning their home.

"At the Tourist Office," Madame Reynaud said, squeezing some lemon into her tea.

"Why?"

"Because," Madame Reynaud said, not sure how or where to pick the next words to say, "I've been thinking that although you might not need a job, you might want a job."

"There are many reasons to have a job," Monique offered.

"Yes, many reasons."

"I think I would be good at helping people with the maps."

"Very good indeed," Madame Reynaud said with enthusiasm. "You know the tiny streets of Avignon better than anyone, Valerie has said so herself. And you are patient," she added, nodding her head. "That is your gift. You are patient. A job like that, helping people find their way around with just a little map will take a great deal of patience."

Monique was so stunned, she completely forgot to tell her mother she had invited Monsieur Boffard to come to their home tomorrow at six for aperitifs.

Monique sat at her dressing table brushing her short dark curls. There was much to think about and much to do before Monday when she would go to the tourist office to ask for a job. She was so excited she could hardly sit still, the brush flitted and jumped in her hand like a bird, as she alternately smoothed and fluffed her hair wondering which way it looked best. She would have to ask André. She hoped André was right about the cane: that the two of them carried each other well.

A GARDEN WALL IN PROVENCE

She needed to forget about the cane. It didn't matter anymore. What mattered was what she could do. She could type, she could speak French, of course, and also a little German and English.

She knew every side street and short cut in Avignon. She knew which buses went where and when. She knew where the museums were as well as the restaurants and the fancy clothing stores. She knew the little ins and outs of the winding streets of the zone piétons as well as who sold the best nougat and who had the freshest cakes and bread.

She held her breath a moment, sat up straight and looked at her thin reflection in the mirror. There had been so many nights she had gone to bed wishing for a job. In all the years of wishing, she never let herself really believe this day would come.

She could hear the mistral blow and whistle through their garden. It was the mistral that blew this good fortune her way. She could feel it in her bones. She could hardly wait to see André tomorrow and tell him of all that had happened in these past few days since her mother had borrowed Madame Giroux's fine fur coat for her and she had gotten her hair cut.

The words of the Gypsy woman had frightened Madame Reynaud. They were harsh words, the way truth is often harsh, and she was afraid to go to sleep. Madame Reynaud smoothed the deep fold of the top sheet with her hands and lay flat on her back, staring at her bedroom ceiling. Monique would leave her. She had known it to be true for so many years, yet had tricked herself into believing Monique couldn't possibly have the strength to go out on her own.

It was like knowing you would die. Of course, you knew you would die one day, but because it was so true, so inevitable, you were able to push the thought back, back into some quiet corner of your mind that only bothered you when you couldn't sleep.

And this afternoon, she believed, if she got enough flowers in the house, if she filled every corner with color and light and sweet memories of the past, the prospect of letting Monique go wouldn't be so frightening, and she would be able to tell Monique she could have a life of her own.

Even with all the beautiful flowers, the prospect of losing her daughter was frightening and sad and lonely making. She had let her tea get cold while she talked about it, because she knew if she touched her cup, her hands would shake, making the cup and saucer rattle like ghost bones, and Monique would not be able to hear that she had her blessing and could at last leave.

Monique. Dear, sweet, Monique who had been so patient. Monique who had sat by her father's bedside the whole time he was sick, and when he died had stayed without being asked, keeping her company all these years, and never once complained.

The Gypsy woman's words pounded in Madame Reynaud's heart, and their meaning was clear: Madame Reynaud had not cared for Monique, but instead, Monique had cared for her. But it was done now. She had said what she had been so afraid all these years to say, and Monique was free.

Over cold tea, they had talked about how Monique could ride the bus to work, taking her lunch some days so she could sit in the park in the sunshine while she ate. And how, maybe once a week or so, they could meet at the little cafe in the Place des Corps Saints, or when it was raining go to Le Chandlier, or one of the fancy places on the Rue Joseph Vernet and have lunch together.

Madame Reynaud could imagine a map with all of Monique's favorite restaurants marked neatly in ink, as though Monique had been making plans to go to work and have lunch with her mother for years.

It was done, as it should have been done years ago. And now, Madame Reynaud could only hope the Gypsy woman was right about Monsieur Boffard.

SUNDAY

When Monique opened her eyes, she could hear her mother down in the kitchen putting on the tea kettle.

"Bonjour," Monique sang out from her bed.

"Bonjour, ma petite," Madame Reynaud called back. "Tea?"

"But, of course," Monique answered, rolling to her side in order to push herself upright, swinging her legs over the edge of her bed and her feet into her slippers.

"Need some help coming downstairs?"

"No," Monique answered, pulling her arms into her robe and tossing her new short hair with her fingers so the curls could shake themselves free from her long night's sleep. "I'll be there in a minute."

Madame Reynaud took the good china down from the top shelf of the buffet and began to set the table. She had already put out her best white linen cloth and linen napkins, along with a small vase of roses on the table and had arranged butter, jam, fresh lemon, cream and sugar by each of their places as though they were dining at the fanciest restaurant in Avignon. With the good china on the table, all she needed to do was put the croissants and brioche on a platter, pour the juice and serve the fruit.

"This looks like breakfast for a king," Monique exclaimed when she saw the table.

"For a queen," Madame Reynaud corrected. "Now sit, and let your birthday begin. Tea?"

"Oui, Madame."

"The grapefruit looked quite firm this morning at the market, so I bought one for us to share."

"You've already been to the market?"

"And to Monsieur Boffard's for croissants and brioche."

"Madame Fleury is still ill?"

"On the contrary, she is quite well. Did you know I tried to buy croissants from Monsieur Boffard the other day and he wouldn't let me?"

"You didn't tell me."

"Well, it is true. I kept insisting I wanted some, but he wouldn't let me buy any, saying they weren't good enough. Can you ever remember Madame Giroux refusing to sell us something?"

"No, now that you mention it, I cannot."

"Neither can I. Which just goes to show you that Monsieur Boffard is a fine boulanger. Here," Madame Reynaud said, pulling off the curved tip of one of the croissants, "isn't it delicate?"

"Yes," Monique answered.

"And sweet?"

"Yes."

"As I have said, he is a fine boulanger. And just look at the brioche, so plump and golden. Monsieur Boffard insisted I take them. He wouldn't let me pay. Taste," she said to Monique, pinching off a piece from the fluted edges. "They are as fine as any we have ever had, am I right?"

"It is very good."

"One needs a good brioche to chase away the mistral. When I went to Monsieur Boffard's this morning, I met Monsieur Duncan walking Pantagruel. When the wind came from behind in an attempt to knock everyone off the sidewalks, Monsieur Duncan had to hold tight to Pantagruel's leash. The two of them stood anchored as though they were welded together to keep from blowing away."

"Pantagruel has brought some new life to our quiet little neighborhood," Monique said, realizing that had it not been for Pantagruel, the whole situation with Monsieur Boffard might not have ever happened.

"It is good Monsieur Duncan has agreed to take him for walks, for I fear Madame Pécaut would have let the wind chase her into her house and Pantagruel would have been forced to do his barking and running in her yard."

"The wind sounds sweet compared to Pantagruel's growling."

"But, he is a good dog."

"I agree," replied Monique.

The two women were silent for a moment while Madame Reynaud stirred sugar into her tea, and Monique picked the crust away from the end of her croissant.

"It has been quite a week," Monique said idly as she nibbled at the sweet bread.

"So much has happened! I have been meaning to tell you how pretty you look with your new short hair! It will be perfect for your job at the tourist office."

"If I get the job."

"I am sure you will. How could you not?"

"I hope you are right," replied Monique

"You never told me about your haircut," Madame Reynaud said, taking a sip of tea, getting ready to hear Monique's story.

"Or about André or Monsieur Boffard," Monique added.

"André?"

"He is the one who cut my hair. He's coming this evening at six to take me out for an aperitif for my birthday. Which," Monique hesitated a moment before continuing, "happens to be the same time I have invited Monsieur Boffard ... "

"But, I have invited Monsieur Boffard!"

"You have?"

"Of course, for your fête."

"What fête?"

"For your birthday. Madame Pécaut, Madame and Monsieur Duprés, Madame Fleury, Madame and Monsieur Giroux and Monsieur Boffard, they are all coming. Oh dear!" As Madame Reynaud called off the list, she realized for the first time that everyone she had invited was old. "I have been a fool," she said, reaching out across the table to take her daughter's hand, "to believe I was making a party for you. The truth is, I was making a party for myself."

"But Monsieur Boffard believes he has been invited to have a drink alone with you."

"Then he will be quite surprised."

"You are not angry?"

"About André?" Madame Reynaud asked.

"About Monsieur Boffard."

"I should be angry, but as you can see, I have also invited him to come."

"I only meant to help."

"I think you should tell me about André."

"He is very tall and thin," Monique said.

"Is he handsome?" Madame Reynaud asked.

"Not so handsome as he is kind. He knew immediately that Madame Giroux's coat was not mine."

"Ah, the coat!" Madame Reynaud said, shaking her head. "I think I'm going to like this André."

Monique had insisted she help her mother prepare for the fête, which had not been Madame Reynaud's intention, but she gave in, realizing that letting Monique help her was the only way to allow Monique to enjoy the party she would not be attending. One case of the Gigondas had been pulled from beneath the staircase, and six bottles had been selected for the fête.

"Will six be enough?" Monique asked, carrying the bottles one at a time into the dining room to be put on the buffet next to their best red wine glasses.

"I should think so," Madame Reynaud responded. "Surely if we drank more we would all have trouble finding our way home."

"But Monsieur Duprés will be here and, of course Madame Fleury, who has a tendency to get an itchy throat when good wine is around."

"There will also be Monsieur Boffard."

"Eight bottles?" Monique asked, opening the case again.

"To be safe, eight."

"Will you serve the quiche and rillettes at the table?"

"I believe that would be best. We are too old to stand around balancing a drink in one hand and a slice of something in the other while trying to be polite and make conversation. Besides, if Madame Fleury and Madame Pécaut start to argue about anything, it would better for my china and crystal for everyone to be sitting down. We'll need grandmother's plates for the quiche and rillettes. I'd like to use the pretty cut glass plates for the gâteaux."

"Do you think Madame Fleury will have forgotten about her lost shepherd before Monsieur Duprés arrives?" Monique asked.

"One can only hope. It is not easy getting old; things get stuck in your mind, and you cannot always forget what should be forgotten."

"I regret I had forgotten to tell you about André and Monsieur Boffard."

"It is as it should be."

Madame Reynaud sat on the edge of her bed listening to Monique move around downstairs. Monique had not wanted André to come while she was upstairs. She did not want him to see her make her slow careful way down the staircase, so she had dressed an hour earlier and was now downstairs waiting. Madame Reynaud could hear her fiddling with this and that, letting whatever little task she could find fill the nervous moments before André arrived.

It had been a fine day, the two of them working together to prepare for the fête. Monique was, as she had always been, calm yet cautious, always aware of Madame Reynaud's needs. If Madame Reynaud had only had the strength, she would have forced Monique to seek her independence earlier, but she had not.

"Should I heat some water to warm the silver teapot?" Monique called up from the bottom of the stairs.

"Yes," Madame Reynaud called back, knowing as she did it was really too soon to do so but that Monique needed something to busy herself with while she waited for André to arrive. "Wrap it in a towel to keep it warm."

"The coffee pot also?"

"Yes," Madame Reynaud answered, letting her feet pull free of her slippers.

Her husband's slippers were worn so badly, the places where her toes had rested these last ten years were now thin as paper. When she slid her feet across the floor, she could feel the cold rise up from the grey tiles as if she were walking barefoot in a graveyard. It was time to move on.

"Are you almost dressed?" Monique called out from the kitchen. "It's nearly six, they'll be here any minute."

"I'm coming," Madame Reynaud said as she heard Monsieur Boffard whistling down their street as he walked towards their house.

She slipped on her good navy heels to come downstairs.

"Bonne fête et bonne soirée," Monsieur Boffard called out behind their closed front door.

Before Monique could let go of the last latch and pull the handle to let him in, the wind blew the door open and there stood Monsieur Boffard, his head thrown back like Father Christmas, his great paw of a hand wrapped around the thin line of André's shoulder.

"You cannot always listen to what a woman has to say," he bellowed, enjoying the sound of his own laugh as it pushed against the tight little walls of Madame Reynaud and Monique's home. "Sometimes they say no when they mean yes. Sometimes they scowl when they really want to laugh. Am I right, Madame Reynaud?" he asked, his eyes twinkling, as he drew his other arm from behind his back and held out a wild bouquet of creamy white lilies and dark red roses all tangled together with slender stalks of freesia and fragrant stems of eucalyptus.

"Bonsoir, Monsieur Boffard," Madame Reynaud blushed. She was dumbstruck by the size of the bouquet and the brashness of Monsieur Boffard's true words.

"Bonsoir, Mademoiselle Reynaud," he greeted Monique in mock formality.

"Bonsoir, Monsieur Boffard," offered Monique. "I see you have met my friend, André."

"Oui, and a fine friend he is! I was just telling him," Monsieur Boffard continued, "that a beautiful woman is like the mistral. She can look as if she cares about nothing," he said, pointing to the endless smooth blanket of blue in the evening sky, "but inside, there is always something raging. And, if you are lucky," he laughed as the wind chose that very moment to race down their small alleyway and push the two men through the open front door. "What's raging is love."

POST SCRIPT:

WHERE THIS STORY CAME FROM

In 1991 our family lived in a tight little row house at 12 Impasse de l'Alliance in Avignon, France. My husband, Jeff, was on sabbatical from North Carolina State University in Raleigh, and I had a contract to write a series of articles about cooking and eating in France for a regional food magazine back home. It was a great year. Our two older children attended the local school down the street (and, yes, it had a big green door that opened into a courtyard where the children played at recess), and our youngest child, who was only three months old when we landed in Avignon, stayed home with us.

Every morning, Jeff would wake up early in order to go out to buy bread for breakfast at our favorite local bakery, Guy's. If it was Wednesday, the day that Guy's was closed, we, like all good people in our neighborhood (we were told by our neighbors that Guy's made the best bread, and we agreed), were forced to eat what we all believed was inferior bread from the boulanger down the street. The bread from the other boulanger was said to be industrial bread, unlike Guy's artisanal bread. Eating any bread other than the good bread from Guy's was considered a hardship among those who lived on the Impasse de l'Alliance. God forbid some unforeseen tragedy might strike and both stores would be closed on the same day and we would be forced to succumb to going to the grocery store to buy bread. Had we done so, I'm sure there would have been an uproar.

There are boulangeries in just about every neighborhood in France. And, in all neighborhoods, there is a prearranged agreement among the boulangers as to what days they should be open and what days they should be closed, so everyone who lives within a short walk can have fresh bread every day for every meal. Also, every boulanger normally extends the courtesy of letting the closest butcher and green grocer know when he plans to close his shop for vacation so that they can vacation at the same time. It goes without saying that you buy your meat and your vegetables from the shop closest to your preferred bakery; thus, if your bakery is closed, you would move all your business down the street to the other boulanger, butcher and green grocer all clustered together. In short, as a neighborhood merchant, if the bakery closest to your shop is closed for vacation, you might as well close up and go to the beach as well because your customers will disappear along with the bread.

Bread is a way of life in France, and the fresh baguette is nearly a sacrament. Most French people go to the bakery not once, but twice, and sometimes three times a day to buy a fresh baguette. Since the bread is made without any preservatives, it is best eaten just hours after it is baked. Any boulanger worth his salt bakes fresh loaves throughout the day so his customers can have a fresh loaf for lunch and dinner as well as for breakfast. Anything less on the part of the baker would be considered shameful.

Our little home was one of a row of homes on Impasse de l'Alliance. Like Monique and Madame Reynaud's home, our neighbors could open their bedroom windows and see down into our backyard and garden and keep tabs on our comings and goings. I know we provided much gossip amongst our neighbors. However, they gave as good as they got, and I left Avignon with great stories to tell!

There was a laundromat at the end of the street where the Gypsies, who camped on the edge of Avignon, would come from time to time to wash enormous amounts of laundry. While the old Gypsy woman in her big skirts and arms full of gold bracelets wrestled the mounds of dirty clothing from washer to dryer, and back into the huge sacks and woven baskets in which she had hauled them into the laundry, the two men who always accompanied her would sit on old wooden chairs in the bed of their big truck, smoking and talking.

We had a small washing machine at our home, but no dryer. And, although I had a clothesline outside where I usually hung clothes to dry, on days when it rained, or on days when the wash for three young children and two adults was just too much, I would go to the laundromat.

I would usually take our youngest son, Cole, with me when I went to do the wash. One morning, as Jeff was leaving to buy bread for our breakfast, our neighbor opened her front bedroom window and yelled down to him: "You should not let her go to the laundromat when the Gypsies are there! The Gypsy woman will steal your baby!"

Jeff tried to reassure her that both the baby and I would be fine. Not willing to let her concern be brushed aside, she continued: "And

A GARDEN WALL IN PROVENCE

tell your wife she should not wear her good earrings either! The Gypsy woman will snatch them out of her ears before your wife will even know what is happening!"

Despite her warning, I continued to go to the laundromat with Cole and continued to wear the only pair of earrings I had brought with me to France. Not surprisingly, given the fear of the Gypsies and the advance notice they always gave the neighbors of their arrival as their old, battered flatbed truck ground its gears to a halt along the curb of Impasse de l'Alliance, I was often the only other person in the laundromat when the Gypsy woman did the wash. The owner, who usually sat on one of the plastic chairs and smoked cigarette after cigarette as he gossiped with the neighborhood women while they did their wash, would hide in his office when the Gypsies came.

Over time, the old Gypsy woman became comfortable with me taking up one or two of the washing machines, and sometimes we would talk. Between her Romany-studded patois and my very elementary French, if we spoke slowly to each other, we could hold a conversation. One rainy afternoon, when the two Gypsy men had retreated to the cab of the truck to smoke and sleep, she dared to sit next to me and show me the heavy locket she kept on a gold chain around her neck. In a whisper, she opened the locket to show me a picture of a beautiful blue-eyed boy of about eight or ten. On one side of the locket was his picture and on the other was a small curl of his dark brown hair.

Her son had died in some horrible accident when he was still a child, and she had cut the curl from his head when she prepared him for burial. So, there we were, just two mothers with their sons: mine

119

asleep in his stroller, and hers caught forever in a gold locket.

To say our neighbors kept tabs on our young family is an understatement. Somehow, they knew nearly everything about us without us ever having had a conversation beyond hello and goodbye. Fortunately, I was able to take the intrusion into our privacy as just part of living in this enchanting world of daily bread.

One of the most telling and funny things about this neighborly concern happened the day my mother-in-law came from the United States for a visit.

My mother-in-law was flying into Paris and didn't want to take the train alone from Paris to Avignon, so Jeff took the train up to meet her and bring her back. The night before he left to pick up his mother, I had served a roast chicken for dinner, and there were leftovers, but not enough to make a second meal for the next evening when Jeff and his mother would arrive. As planned, Jeff left early to take the high speed TGV to Paris, so I took our two older children, Neil and Hedy, to school. Afterwards, I went with Cole to the butcher shop around the corner from our house. It was early in the morning, and the shop was crowded with mothers buying meat and putting in their orders for dinner. Most French homes do not have ovens, or at least not very big ones. Why would you need an oven if you never had to bake? So, if you wanted to cook a large roast or have a roasted chicken or even a pork loin, you would go early to the butcher, put in your order, have him cook it for you on his big rotisserie. It would then be ready for you when you picked up your children from school later that afternoon or when you came home from work.

I had planned to serve the leftover chicken to Neil and Hedy and myself and to make chopped steak for Jeff and his mother. I had decided I would also serve sautéed vegetables and a salad with the meal and finish off the evening with a fresh baguette and some cheese.

Because the tiny butcher shop was quite crowded and I had Cole in a backpack, I stood at the rear of the store so I wouldn't accidently knock into anyone. When Monsieur Dudie, the butcher, saw me, he pointed at me to give my order.

"Two hundred grams of steak haché," I called out.

A hush went over the chattering shop. Madame Dudie looked at her husband in disbelief. Monsieur Dudie surveyed the quiet crowd.

"Two hundred grams?" he asked.

"Oui, two hundred grams," I responded.

His hand swept across the crowd as they turned to look at me.

"Incredible! Her husband has gone to Paris to pick up his mother. This woman has two growing children, a baby, her mother-in-law and her husband to feed tonight, and all she asks for is two hundred grams of steak haché!"

People began shaking their heads. I reached into my purse searching for my French dictionary hoping desperately to be able to quickly find the French word for leftovers.

There was no such word.

"Two hundred grams!" he loudly announced a second time. Everyone in the shop stopped talking and shook their heads in disbelief.

I was caught.

"Five hundred grams," I called out in desperation.

"Ahhh, five hundred grams," Messieurs Dudie said nodding to the now murmuring crowd as he dug out a nice lean chunk of beef from his display case and stuffed it into the grinder. "And, how are you going to cook it?" he asked.

My first lesson about the relationship between daily life in France and French food/cooking came when we moved into our little home. We did not have an oven but we did have three small electric burners and a small countertop rotisserie I never turned on because I wasn't sure how to use it. In truth, it was a complicated machine with many moving parts and gadgets that I had no desire ever to clean, so I avoided getting it dirty at all costs.

In addition to the rotisserie, I had an electric kettle for heating water for tea. We didn't have a dishwasher, but instead, we had a tiny sink right under a small kitchen window that looked out onto the quiet sidewalk along Impasse de l'Alliance.

Of the good news/bad variety, there was plenty of counter space in my tiny kitchen because there was no full size Western style refrigerator taking up part of the room. Instead, there was a small under-the-counter refrigerator just slightly larger than a standard dorm refrigerator. The size of this refrigerator, along with its lack of freezer, was then key to my new life.

The refrigerator was just large enough to hold the fresh fruits, vegetables and dairy products I would need for our family for one day and no more; therefore, I had to shop every day. In short, I no longer had the U.S. luxury of making a shopping list for the week's one big trip to the grocery store. Instead, I had the French luxury of taking a walk every morning around the neighborhood to gather what I would need for that day.

As I mentioned before, where you buy your bread also determines where you buy your meat, vegetables and cheese for the day. And, as in my novella, loyalty plays a big part of life in the community. I did not fully understand all of this when we first arrived in Avignon.

In the beginning, I did my shopping in Avignon much the same way I shopped in Raleigh. Because we were a family of five on a tight budget, I'd look for the best deals, buying strawberries from one place and carrots and salad fixings from another, depending on who had the best produce and the best deal. This seemed fine, except I couldn't find parsley anywhere in any of the stores, despite the fact that almost every woman I passed on the street had a beautiful bouquet of parsley stuck in the top of her shopping bag.

Wanting fresh parsley, I kept looking, going from one market to the next. Clearly, there was some great herb store somewhere I hadn't yet found, and I just needed to persevere. However, whenever I would ask for parsley at each new market I went to, my trusty French dictionary in hand, the grocer would inevitably look at me like I was either speaking some ancient lost language or had simply lost my mind.

Then one day, the mystery was solved. The weather was dreary and threatening to rain, so I decided to forgo my usual morning of foraging from one shop to another and, instead, to stop by the market close to the children's school to get clementines because they were on special in that store that morning. Afterwards, I went to the market at the top of our street to do the rest of my shopping for the day. One of the women from our neighborhood was standing in line in front of me at the second shop. I had seen her at this particular market before, so I was not surprised to see her there that morning. What did surprise me, however, was that after she paid for her groceries, the grocer reached under the counter and handed her a beautiful bundle of bright green parsley.

"Pour vous, un petit cadeau," he said, smiling sweetly.

And, just as sweetly, she thanked him and tucked the parsley into the top of her basket.

At last, I understood: fresh parsley, that most important ingredient in good French cooking, was not something you could buy with money. Instead, it was the reward you got from being loyal to one green grocer over the others.

I also understood that I would not be getting any parsley that day because the grocer could see by the bag I was carrying that I had already purchased clementines from his competitor down the street.

It took me a week of deciding which of the four green grocers near our home was the best and the one I would claim as my own, and another week of showing my loyalty to that grocer by only shopping with him before the shop keeper took my money, handed me my change, and, then, after I smiled and thanked him, reached down below the counter and handed me my petit cadeau, my little gift.

Like all the good French women who lived in Avignon, I learned I should tuck that parsley into the top of my bag or my shopping basket in order to show it off to the other grocers as I walked by their shops. It was a sign that I was not only loyal, but also was playing by the rules.

I never went without parsley again.

As for the mistral, the violent and cold wind is both fierce and mysterious and is much talked about in Provence. They say it comes from Siberia. It is accompanied by clear, fresh weather and seems to come out of nowhere with an average speed of fifty kilometers an hour but has been known to reach speeds of more than ninety kilometers an hour. It usually blows in winter or spring but can occur at any season. It frequently lasts for several days and sometimes for more than a week.

The combination of a beautiful clear blue sky and the fierce and seemingly unending wind is unnerving. The cold wind cuts through you. It rushes and whistles down the alleyways and streets, tearing your laundry from the clotheslines and rattling your shutters. The constant noise combined with the anxiety that it might last for days is enough to give anyone a headache. Everyone complains.

I didn't understand the power of the mistral the first time it came. Afterwards, I understood, since it tore some wash off our line and forced our children to play inside until it left. Seeing how terrible, fierce and unforgiving it could be, stealing both our laundry, our playtime, and our sleep, had it hurt one of my children like it had hurt Madame Reynaud's child, I would fear it and hate it the rest of my life. Having experienced it, I also understood how Monique would feel compelled to fight it for her freedom.

Our ten months in Avignon gave me a taste for good bread, an appreciation for high garden walls, a curiosity about Gypsies, and a hunger for the pleasure of a simple life with a small kitchen that would force me to slow down and take time to wander around gathering what I would need to feed my family, as if that one act was the most important thing I would do all day.

Shortly after we returned to Raleigh, one of our local grocery stores bought a big rotisserie oven and began roasting chickens. I took it as a sign that I should hold fast to the lessons we learned in Avignon about living a good life. I have never baked a chicken again!

Now, if I could only get a boulanger to open a shop around the corner from our home so I could have fresh bread every morning.

A WORD OR TWO ABOUT GOOD
BREAD AND SOME RECIPES

There is really nothing better than being able to walk down your block and into a bakery to buy a loaf of fresh crusty bread for breakfast and another later in the afternoon to have with wine and cheese after your evening meal. Even though there is a resurgence of artisanal bakeries across the United States, there are few cities with a good bakery every few blocks as there still are throughout France and many of the other European countries.

Store bought bread just isn't in the same league as freshly baked artisanal bread. Part of the reason is the preservatives. Others argue that store bought bread isn't good because of the heavily milled flours used by factory-based bakeries. Some purists believe bad bread comes from bad water. In fact, if you are trying to create your own sour dough starter, many bread books suggest you use distilled rather than tap water.

The French would argue that bread should only be made from water, flour, yeast and salt. Period. Because French bakers use no preservatives or any other ingredients that could extend the shelf life of their bread, a good baguette should be eaten within just a few hours after it comes from the oven. After even just a few hours, especially after a loaf has been broken apart or cut, the bread quickly dries out and becomes stale. This is why the French leave their homes to go to the bakery to buy bread not once, not even twice, but often three times a day: for breakfast, lunch and dinner.

A stale loaf of good French bread, however, is far from a tragedy, it is an opportunity to make pain perdu: French toast! Many French bakeries and cafes serve a delicious pain perdu put together much in the same way we would make bread pudding (cutting the bread into cubes, soaking them in a divine mixture of eggs, cream, honey, almonds and cinnamon, then baking them in either a loaf pan or a Bundt pan) sliced like cake and served warm or cold with a generous dollop of whipped cream.

If you don't happen to have a good bakery within walking or even driving distance of your home, you are left having to fend for yourself.

I have a confession to make. I am a decent cook, but not a good baker. My lack of baking skills comes from my lack of willingness to read and follow directions and a certain amount of impatience. Cooking is a rather forgiving and creative endeavor that offers fairly immediate gratification and a great deal of latitude from a pinch of salt to whatever else you happen to have sitting in your fridge that you might be able to throw into the pot to make a hearty soup.

Baking requires many steps, many measurements, rules, rising and waiting times, and a rather strict definition of what something should not only taste like, but also what it should look like when you pull it out of the oven and put it on a plate.

A GARDEN WALL IN PROVENCE

In deciding to include recipes for a decent loaf of French bread as well as a gâteau des rois (the closest you are going to find to a gâteau des rois in the United States will be a New Orleans-style King's Cake), I wanted to find recipes that anyone, or at least anyone interested in trying to learn how to make bread, could pull off successfully.

If you go online and read the various recipes for French baguette you will find everything from a recipe that will take two days and multiple risings to a now popular no-knead bread you quickly throw together and let rise overnight before baking. Some of the recipes are so daunting I decided that if I found them too detailed and scary to even try, you wouldn't try them either. To my mind, this would defeat the purpose of putting a recipe in the book.

If you've never made bread before, the easy recipes I've included here are worth a try.

I wanted readers to be successful with their first loaf of homemade bread, so I pulled out all my recipe books, watched a dozen videos and in the end took my husband's (he is a terrific bread baker) standard bread recipe for Cuban rolls and tried to see how to modify it to bring it as close to French baguette standards as possible.

Here's what's wrong with most recipes you will find in other books: they take too much time. I don't know about you, but I rarely decide the night before to whip up a batch of bread dough so it can rise overnight and I can come home the next day after work and bake it off to serve with a homemade soup or whatever for dinner. That's just not how it goes in my life.

For good measure I'm going to give you two recipes. The first is the recipe for my husband's wonderful Cuban rolls. He got this recipe from our dear friend Alice Lepie, who had adapted it from an old James Beard recipe. Alice died much too young. I love that we got the recipe from Alice because every time we have this bread, we think about her and miss her. Food is a wonderful memory, and Alice's bread is a reminder of all the meals we have shared with people we have loved.

With a few modifications I learned from watching all the videos and reading the various, quite serious "this is how you make real French baguettes" recipes, I think I've created a fairly passable, and for sure easy way to put a good loaf of "French" bread on your table.

The second recipe is one that was passed on to me by a friend whose sister worked in a restaurant where it was her job to come in early everyday and whip up this bread. It's a no-rise bread. From start to finish, it takes less than an hour and a half. It's a very quick and easy bread to make, so easy, that I have made it a hundred times over the years. I love it because it is forgiving and simple and takes no time at all, in fact, considerably less time than the modified Cuban rolls. It can be made shaped into loaves. You can mash it into a flat circle, poke holes in it with your fingers, cover it with salt and herbs and a generous dribble of olive oil and turn it into a delicious focaccia. Or, you can pat it out flat with your hands, spread it with butter, brown sugar, cinnamon, walnuts and raisins, roll it up, slice it into pinwheels, fit the pinwheels tightly together in a baking pan then top it with pats of butter and brown sugar and bake it as cinnamon rolls.

Like its cousins, the French baguette and Alice's Cuban rolls, it has no preservatives and is best eaten the day it is baked.

A Decent Fairly Easy Homemade French Baguette (adapted from James Beard's Cuban Rolls recipe)

Dissolve 1 T. yeast in 2 C. warm water
Stir in 1 T. sugar
Let proof for 15 minutes
Add 1 1/4 t. salt
Mix in 5-7 C. white flour (use bread flour if possible)
Knead (machine kneading is fine) until bread is no longer tacky, but not yet stiff (do not force more flour once dough is no longer tacky)
Let rise 1 1/2 to 2 hours until doubled, in slightly oiled bowl, covered. Preheat oven to 475 degrees (begin preheating well enough in advance to allow oven time to reach this high temperature).
Remove dough from bowl by first loosening it with a spatula around the edge of the bowl. Let it slide from the bowl onto your counter or work surface.

NOTE: I use a large plastic cutting mat on my counter when I work with bread or pastries. It is similar to the ones quilters use for cutting fabric. I bought mine at a hardware store. You can also find them at fabric or art supply stores. They're great to work on and save your countertops.

Cut the dough into 3 somewhat equal pieces. Your goal is to shape but not overwork the dough. Working with one piece at a time, gently press out the dough into a long thin rectangle using your fingertips or the heels of your hands. Once you have a rectangle that's roughly 15" X 5", begin at the top of the long edge of the rectangle and roll the dough forward creating a long thick rope shape. Using the heel of your hand, gently press the edges of the bread dough together, sealing the loaf together and roll the ends of the dough into a point. The long thin loaves should now be approximately 16 inches long.

Sprinkle cornmeal across the bottom of a large baking sheet and place the three pieces of shaped dough side by side but not touching (allow 2-3 inches between each).

Let stand 5 minutes, covered.

Boil some water.

Make 5 or 6 diagonal cuts across the tops of each loaf with either a fresh razor blade or a very sharp knife.

Brush the tops of the loaves with cold water.

Place the baking sheet on the middle shelf of your oven and place a pan of the boiling water on the shelf below.

Spray the inside of the oven with an atomizer (2-3 good squirts of cool water) before you close the oven door.

After the first ten minutes of baking, open the oven and spray again (2-3 good squirts) with cool water.

Bake for a total of 15-20 minutes until loaves are nicely, but not overly browned.

(**Note:** If you have a convection oven, you will find that it will take more like 15 minutes, while a conventional oven will take closer to 20 minutes.)

Remove bread from the cookie sheet while still hot.

Allow the bread to cool for a few minutes before slicing. Serve warm with lots of butter. Enjoy!

Tuscan Bread

Note: This bread's great virtue is that it doesn't require a rising and can be made in little more than an hour from start to out of the oven. Like most single rise quick breads, this one becomes stale quite quickly, which is a good excuse to enjoy it warm with friends!

Mix the following ingredients together in a bowl. In bread jargon, this is called a sponge. Let this mixture sit so it can proof (that is, so you can observe bubbles forming providing proof that the yeast is active and will help your bread rise) for 15 minutes:

1/2 C bread flour

2 T (or 2.25 oz packages) yeast

1/2 C warm water

Add to proofed sponge:

1 T salt (or less to taste)

1 3/4 C warm water

5 C bread flour (more or less as needed)

At this point, if you plan to serve it with soup or a salad, you can add herbs such as rosemary or dill to the dough. I usually add at least one tablespoon of dried herbs to the bread, depending on what I'm pairing the bread with in the meal. Dill is good, and I think some finely chopped fresh rosemary is particularly nice.

Knead and add flour as needed to keep the dough from being too sticky. Continue to knead for 10 minutes or 800-1000 times (If you use bread hook on your mixer to do the kneading, do it for 8-10 minutes to mix and knead thoroughly.)

Divide dough in half. Then, flatten each part onto floured board with rolling pin to half-inch thickness, shaping into a rectangle.

Roll the flattened dough jellyroll style into a loaf, lengthwise. Close up the jellyroll using the heel of your hand (same directions as the French bread recipe). Place each of the finished rolls onto a greased cookie sheet.

Bake 30 minutes at 400° F. Serve hot.

Variation: This dough can be used to make cinnamon rolls. For this purpose:

Omit optional herbs, instead add 1 Tbs of some cinnamon to dough before you begin kneading

Do not divide dough in half

Roll the kneaded dough thinner in one large elongated rectangle.

After rolling out thin, dot with butter and sprinkle with cinnamon and sugar. (I like to use brown sugar for this: ½ C brown sugar and 2 Tbs. cinnamon mixed together. You can also add 1 C of raisins or walnuts, or both!)

Roll up into long roll, closing the ends again with the heel of your hand.

Slice the dough into ½ inch thick pinwheel slices.

Place each pinwheel cut side down on greased cookie sheet with a bit of room for expansion between each pinwheel and bake as above.

After baking, ice with confectioner's sugar-milk glaze (add a bit of flavoring to taste, vanilla is good, as is rum or orange).

Serve warm with lots of butter and a pot of hot tea! Great for big crowd at brunch.

Gâteau Des Rois (King's Cake)

(Adapted from http://www.willowday.com/2012/01/fete-du-roi-january-6.html)

Makes two large cakes.

NOTE: If you want to follow in the tradition of crowning a king or queen when you serve your Kings' Cake, you can either place one candied almond into each of the cakes before baking, or a small plastic or ceramic figure (very small...like the little ceramic animals Red Rose Tea used to give away in their boxes of tea). The person who finds the candied almond or figurine in their slice of cake is declared queen or king for the evening and may reign over the festivities of the evening and grant wishes to all in his or her kingdom!

Ingredients/evening

     1 C lukewarm milk

     1 T or l package dry yeast

     1/4 C lukewarm water

     1/2 C sugar

     Salt (a pinch)

     5 C flour

     2 eggs

     1/2 C softened butter

Ingredients/morning

>1/4 C softened butter
>
>3/4 C sugar
>
>1 T cinnamon
>
>½ C seedless raisins
>
>¾ C slivered almonds
>
>1 C chopped dried fruit (I prefer orange peel, but you can use pineapple, cherries or any other dried fruit, or a mixture of your favorites)
>
>1 beaten egg

Evening

Blend the yeast in the water.

Mix together sugar, salt, milk. Add 1 C of flour and the yeast.

Add another 2 C of flour and beat in a bowl until smooth.

Mix in 2 beaten eggs and the butter.

Add the rest of the flour and knead the dough until smooth.

Let the dough rest 5-10 minutes.

Put the dough in a large bowl, cover it with plastic wrap and let it rest in the fridge overnight.

Morning after

Take dough out of refrigerator and, allow it to come to room temperature.

Preheat the oven to 350° F

Divide the dough in two. Using your hands, flatten the dough into two rectangles approximately 15" long and 6" wide.

Reserve ¼ C slivered almonds and 2 T chopped dried fruit.

Mix together butter, sugar, cinnamon, raisins and remaining slivered almonds and chopped dried fruit.

Spread butter mix on the dough.

Gently roll the dough from the top to the bottom like a jelly roll, pinching the dough together on the bottom and bringing the ends together to form a ring. Roll the dough and put the ends together to form a ring. (You will make two rings from the two halves of the dough.)

Note: The dough will be a little sticky. You do not want to force more flour into the dough, and you also don't want to handle the dough too much.

Put the dough rings on a lightly greased baking sheet, and flatten each with the heels of your hands until the rings are approximately 2 inches thick. They should be the same thickness so they cook evenly. Spread the beaten egg over the surface of the dough with a soft kitchen brush. Sprinkle on reserved slivered almonds and chopped dried fruit. Now sprinkle additional sugar, gently coating the top of each ring.

Put in oven at temperature of 180° C (350° F) for 25 minutes (until it begins to brown and knife inserted comes out clean; cover with foil if browning too fast; do not over bake).